BY MEGAN BRYCE

The Reluctant Bride Collection
To Catch A Spinster
To Tame A Dragon
To Wed The Widow
To Tempt The Saint

A Temporary Engagement
Some Like It Charming
Some Like It Ruthless
Some Like It Perfect
Some Like It Hopeless

To Tempt the Saint

THE RELUCTANT BRIDE COLLECTION

BOOK FOUR

BOOK FOUR

MEGAN BRYCE

To Tempt The Saint

The Reluctant Bride Collection, Book Four

ISBN: 1511466472

ISBN-13: 978-1511466479

meganbrycebooks@gmail.com

If you would like to be notified when a new title becomes available, sign up at **meganbryce.com**

To my husband–
Because he's mine and I'm his;
And I don't know why, it just is.

And to Lynn–
Who believed in me first.
Who believes in me always.

London

One

George St. Clair sat smoking his cigar quietly and gazing into the fire. He worried the crumpled letter in his hand back and forth, back and forth.

He'd thought about tossing it into the fire but knew it wouldn't do any good. Not for anybody.

He couldn't unread it. Couldn't undo the actions of his friend.

George could only pray, and since he hadn't done any kind of praying in years, he wasn't about to start on a scab like his friend George Sinclair.

St. Clair choked, not sure whether it was the smoke tickling or the tears threatening or the laughter bubbling.

Only George Sinclair would run off to India with the widow.

Only George Sinclair could do it expecting to arrive at the very end a happily married man with no consequences to pay.

St. Clair thought again about praying. Just a quick,

quiet entreaty to keep his friend safe. And whole. And, God, happy.

Someone, somewhere, should be happy.

But God had never answered any prayer of his, so St. Clair stared into the red and yellow flames licking at his boots and went through the quickly memorized letter again.

> *St. Clair,*
>
> *Hold tight to your breeches because your worst fear has come true. I am going home to India, Elinor by my side.*

Perhaps it wasn't St. Clair's worst fear. Being forced to watch a pack of rabid dogs tear the skin from his friend's flesh sounded just as bad.

> *I'd apologize for leaving without telling you but there was little time and. . .I know you. You would have locked me away to stop me from doing something so foolish.*

He would have.

> *She's worth any price. Love is.*

Love wasn't.

> *May you find a love worth losing.*
>
> *Or if you can't manage that, come visit us in India and we'll find one for you.*
>
> *Your never dutiful friend,*
>
> *Sinclair*

And if the thought of Sinclair and the widow picking out St. Clair's bride for him didn't make him shudder, nothing ever would.

St. Clair tossed the letter into the fire, and then his cigar because the letter hadn't been enough.

He'd found love already.

He'd found a woman who promised to be steady and true. A woman to give him children and a happy home.

A woman with a demure smile and shy eyes. A woman proper and good.

And then she'd been given to someone else.

His only comfort was that she and her husband stayed in the country and he didn't have to see them.

His only comfort was that he'd been young and foolish when he'd given his heart away and could, almost, forgive himself.

His only comfort was that he refused to be comforted.

St. Clair stood, straightening his coat. He watched as the paper curled and turned to ash, watched as the cigar smoked and burned.

When he turned away, he did it with no prayer on his lips, but a curse.

For the widow; for a woman with a demure smile and shy eyes; for every woman who could bring misery to man.

A pox on them all.

Miss Letitia Blackstock did not exist.

Oh, somewhere she surely did. Somewhere she spent her mornings walking sedately and her evenings with her needlework and she was good and kind and proper.

The kind of young woman who always obeyed her father and listened to her mother and was kind to her younger sisters.

Honora Kempe had met one or two or a dozen Miss Blackstocks in her lifetime, and though Honora had found them all boring, had chosen to become one this time. For this endeavor.

Next time she would pick someone with a little more spirit and spunk.

But, she was Miss Letitia Blackstock for a little while longer so she simpered a smile and batted her eyelashes and quoted the bible as if Miss Blackstock's father was a vicar instead of the tea dealer she imagined him to be.

Some parts of her were harder to hide than others and Honora found bible quoting to be one of those things. Inappropriate bible quoting, at that.

Honora had decided that Miss Letitia Blackstock might be a bit simple-minded because she just didn't have the spite that went with taking scripture out of context on purpose.

Honora Kempe had spite aplenty. Spite and intelligence.

And a forgettable appearance that let her wield that spite and intelligence against the sons of the middle class again and again.

Miss Blackstock, tonight, waved her fan and listened rapturously to a bookseller's youngest son as he pontificated.

He liked to think he was getting somewhere with her, and he might have been if he hadn't kept interrupting her conversation with his practiced diatribes.

No woman liked to be interrupted when she was speaking. Especially when she had a particularly useful scripture to wield.

Blessed are the meek; for they shall inherit the earth. Matthew 5:5.

But she had no opportunity to share it and when the bookseller's youngest son delivered Miss Blackstock back to her aunt and uncle, she curtsied and smiled at him, then forgot about him completely.

Uncle "Hubert" said, "I can't take much more of this."

Aunt "Gertrude" agreed. "I think we should go back to Edinburgh."

Honora waved her fan and kept her Miss Blackstock smile on her face. "We can't go back to Edinburgh, not yet. Not unless you want me married to Mr. Scote in truth."

Aunt Gertrude made a very un-Gertrude-like face, then rallied. "Bath?"

Honora loved Bath. But, again, it would be too soon and she shook her head.

"It will have to be London, I'm afraid."

"I hate London." And it didn't matter which one of them had said it. They both hated London.

Honora didn't enjoy it all that much either.

But the perfect city was impossible. The perfect city was too small and too cloistered and there was nowhere to hide.

But perhaps when Honora grew too old to continue collecting suitors, and when they'd saved enough money that her majesty's five percent gave them a respectable living, perhaps then they could return home again. Return to live near her young siblings and not under her father's thumb and live out her days as a too-odd spinster.

Marriage was not to be for Honora but she liked being engaged. And she enjoyed her engagements while they lasted because, sometimes sooner and sometimes later, they would all end spectacularly. And always by her fiancé because how else could she force him to pay a modest sum for his breach of promise?

She could thank the newspapers for the idea. They adored reporting the goings-on of every poor woman forced to sue when her formerly affianced callously broke off their engagement.

The fact that such a heinous act sentenced the woman to a life of poverty– forevermore unmarried and childless– guaranteed that the courts nearly always gave the woman a nice reward for her suffering.

Those ladies chose to spend it, Honora imagined, walking sedately in the mornings and practicing needlepoint in the evenings and, perhaps, mourning the life they could have had.

Children and a husband.

Honora had already mourned that loss. And no court would ever reward the act that had sentenced *her* to a life of poverty. Forevermore unmarried and childless.

Aunt Gertrude said, "Everyone's talking about Miss Smith and the Earl of Ferrers."

Honora nodded. It was the latest, and greatest, breach of promise suit ever brought to the courts because the lady was asking for a ridiculous £20,000 in damages. She would have been lucky to get a tenth of that.

Uncle Hubert said, "She should have settled out of court. £1000 and she could have had a very comfortable income. In the country."

Honora smiled. "Do you think she could have even got that without taking him to court?"

He nodded. "£100 for a haberdasher or a clerk. £1000 for an earl."

Since they'd got £100 from a haberdasher and £100 from a clerk themselves, Honora had to believe him.

Aunt Gertrude sighed. "Oh, for an earl. One fell swoop and we would be done."

Uncle Hubert fingered his cravat. "And one short misstep and we'd shorten our lives by the length of a rope.

Better to stay away from the landed gentry."

Honora agreed with him. She had no desire to pit herself against the resources of the upper class and no reason to.

It wasn't an earl who'd stolen her life. It wasn't a married man of the landed gentry who had preyed on a young girl's loneliness, naivete, and stupidity, and then left her alone to bear the consequences.

It wasn't the upper classes she would reclaim her life from, one by one, man by man, until she once again had the future she'd been born to.

George St. Clair had taken an interest in steam courtesy of his new-found love of cigars.

Steam ships sailed daily to the west bringing back the fragrantly rolled leaves. His father had sniffed snuff; George smoked cigars.

He and every gentleman he was acquainted with had caught the craze, the papers announcing that this year more than 250,000 pounds of cigars were imported into England. The number continued to rise incredibly not because there were more ships sailing, but because they were faster.

Steam.

His father had watched masted ships head out to cross the ocean, their sails flapping in the winds; George watched coal-powered puffs rising from stacks.

He had no doubt that in a few years they would find a way to send steam-powered ships eastward, cutting the trip to India from six months to a mere six weeks.

He might see his friend again before another eight years

was gone, and St. Clair thought he would enjoy the look on the widow's face should he track them down.

But today, St. Clair was still in England, sitting in the back row of a large lecture hall, listening to the first in a series on the power of steam. At the heat contained in fractured coal that ran like ribbons down the backbone of England.

The only distraction to his thorough enjoyment of the lecture was the sporadic snores emanating from the gentleman asleep in the row in front of him.

St. Clair shifted, grabbing the attention of the woman sitting beside the snorer.

She turned her head just enough so that he could see muddy brown eyes sitting beneath a hideous hat and she whispered, "My uncle. Some of us do not find heat and water so very intriguing."

St. Clair muttered, "Then some of us should leave."

She whispered to her uncle, "*Awake thou that sleepest,*" and then to St. Clair, "Ephesians 5:14."

But the man continued to sleep, and to snore, and she merely shrugged and turned her head forward again.

When the lecture was over, St. Clair stood impatiently and jostled the man into waking before stalking off.

At the next week's lecture, St. Clair stopped as soon as he entered the hall. As soon as he saw a hideous hat placed jauntily over muddy brown eyes. His eyes flicked to the matron sitting beside the woman and he stalked up to say uncharitably, "Is this one going to stay awake?"

The younger woman didn't tip her head up to look at him but nonetheless said conversationally, "Most likely. She's married, therefore has extensive experience staying awake while a man pontificates about a subject she has no interest in."

St. Clair found he had no reply to that.

He stood there looking down at bare twigs sticking out of her hat, then grunted and took his now customary spot.

The older woman did stay awake, taking out her knitting halfway through and *click, click, clicking* through the lecture.

St. Clair did not miss that the longer the clicking continued the wider the younger woman's mouth smiled.

St. Clair glared at the back of her head.

When the lecture was over, and he'd missed one word out of every four, he stood with a huff and left.

He nearly made it out the door before turning around and stomping back to the pair of women.

He growled, "I assume you will be here next week?"

The younger woman looked up then, a demure smile stuck on her face but her eyes jabbing.

"Yes."

"Would you be ever so kind as to sit in the front."

"I don't think so. I like to see the crowd as well as the speaker."

"Well, so do I."

"Oh, good. Then we will see you next week."

The next week, she was indeed sitting right in front of his spot, but this time she'd brought a maid.

St. Clair debated with himself, but then, finally, moved to sit in his accustomed place. He would not be chased off.

Especially not by a woman who murmured *bravo* condescendingly into her leaflet.

George made himself comfortable and said to the back of her hat, "I will not be mocked by a woman I have not been introduced to."

"Very good." She turned slightly in her seat to look at her maid and said, "And since we cannot be introduced, you are protected from my scathing wit. Perhaps I will bring my uncle again next week and we can dispense with the niceties."

St. Clair could only think *Dear God* and *Please, don't* so he said nothing.

The harpy did not heed his silence.

"It doesn't really work, does it? Introductions and societal standing, not when there are too many new people one must interact with. Not when we must decide on appearance alone how we should act toward each other instead of comparing our familial connections."

"Appearance alone is enough. I can tell all I need to about you by those barren twigs sticking haphazardly out of your bonnet. You are a bluestocking from a good enough family."

Her lips tipped up. "Bluestocking? I suppose I can tell all I need to about *you* from that term. But then I remember you've come to learn about the wonders of steam so you must not be so out-of-date and old-fashioned as I imagine."

The lecturer moved toward the dais, shuffling his papers, and George leaned forward quickly. "And I would enjoy being able to actually hear all about steam today. Your maid did not bring her knitting, did she?"

The woman turned her head away from him and back toward the dais. "She will refrain."

"If she snores, I will jab her with my walking stick."

She looked down at her leaflet again. "*Put up again thy sword into his place: for all they that take the sword, shall perish with the sword.* Matthew 26:52."

The surly gentleman sitting behind Honora did not use his walking stick on her poor maid but only because he'd been too narrow in his threat. The maid didn't knit or snore; she fidgeted. And with every fidget came a creak and a moan from her chair.

With every creak and moan came a loud sigh behind her.

Honora was hardly able to hear the lecture with all the moaning and sighing, and she sighed quietly herself.

She really did want to hear all about the wonders of steam, and she was running out of companions. Uncle Hubert and Aunt Gertrude refused to come again and Honora could hardly blame them. The wonders of steam– pistons and water and coal– were a bit dry.

Honora wouldn't bring her maid again and there was only one other person she could ask to attend with her.

She didn't want to.

She wanted to keep him far away from anything pertaining to Honora Kempe, and Miss Letitia Blackstock would have no reason to be excited about a lecture, about steam.

But she wouldn't be run off by a sour-tempered man.

Especially one who grumbled and sighed and cleared his throat impatiently at her when he rose to leave.

I can tell all I need to about you by those barren twigs sticking haphazardly out of your bonnet.

Honora watched as he stalked out the doors and thought, *No, you don't.*

Halfway through the next week, Miss Letitia Blackstock had her first ever mental excitement. It surprised everyone involved, but Honora the most. Perhaps she had underestimated the girl.

In any event, one morning when the quietly charming and acceptably solicitous Mr. Moffat came to visit, he found her weeping prettily into a handkerchief and fell promptly to his knees.

"Miss Blackstock! You are unwell! Let me call for your aunt at once."

"Oh, Mr. Moffat! I must look a fright."

Miss Blackstock's eyes sparkled from her unshed tears and her nose was nowhere near red since she'd been careful to pat it gently.

Mr. Moffat, ever the courteous gentlemen, said, "You look radiant as always. Please tell me what the matter is."

"It's uncle. He's so tired of hearing about the wedding and the flowers and the trousseau that he says my aunt and I have lost all reason. That we are both too, too silly."

"What else is an engaged woman supposed to talk of but flowers and her trousseau?"

"Steam."

Mr. Moffat sat back on his heels. "Steam?"

"My uncle thinks I should be interested in. . .science. And progress."

"Science? Progress?"

Letitia nodded. "To be well-rounded. You know how he feels about being well-rounded. *The heart of the prudent getteth knowledge; and the ear of the wise seeketh knowledge.* Proverbs 18:15."

Mr. Moffat closed his eyes tightly, the scripture quoting the least favorite feature of his future wife. Miss Blackstock did try to remember but Honora had little hope she would be able to stop.

She said, "There is a series of lectures about steam that he began taking me to but this week he's cried off." Letitia sniffed and stamped her foot. "He thinks I'm silly! I will finish this series to *prove* that I am not. Do you think I'm silly, Mr. Moffat?"

"Of course not. I will take you."

"To the lecture?" she cried, and he preened at her.

"Of course."

She leaned forward to whisper conspiratorially, "It is terribly dull. And the company is. . .objectionable."

He smiled, obviously relieved to hear that she did not actually find steam an invigorating subject. And then he frowned.

"I am sure your uncle would never have let you go in the first place if the company was not respectable."

"Oh, it's respectable. Just. . . sour. But you'll see, when you take me."

And she beamed at him.

They arrived at the lecture hall early and Miss Blackstock gossiped about the attendees, making up stories about them to make Mr. Moffat laugh.

Her maid, to both women's relief, waited outside.

They made their way to their seats, Honora's eyes meeting the surly gentleman's in the next row back long enough for him to say, "Let me guess. Your brother, or a cousin. Is there any hope he will be quiet for the duration of the lecture or will you two be chattering away the entire time?"

Mr. Moffat stopped and turned at the rude intrusion. "Not her brother or her cousin. Her fiancé. Mr. Anthony Moffat of Cheapside. And you are, sir?"

Sourpuss looked completely taken aback and Honora tried not to roll her eyes at him. A woman wears a twig in her hat and the man thinks she's an open book.

Pfft.

He finally said, "Mr. George St. Clair. Of Lancashire."

"And this is Miss Letitia Blackstock. At least for a little while longer."

Mr. Moffat beamed down at her and Miss Blackstock beamed back.

Mr. George St. Clair of Lancashire looked like he wanted to vomit.

She nodded her head at him and said sweetly, "So good to finally meet you, Mr. St. Clair."

He looked even more taken back at her sweet tone and then the skin between his eyes puckered and he narrowed his eyes.

Honora quickly bade Mr. Moffat to sit down and when he did, leaned in to whisper, "Sour."

Mr. Moffat snickered, and Mr. St. Clair sat back in his chair and folded his arms, studying the two of them as if they had suddenly sprouted smoke stacks.

Honora would have enjoyed it more if Mr. Moffat had not then chattered throughout the entire lecture.

Mr. St. Clair stood at the end of it and said loudly, "These lectures are so very illuminating; I wish I could hear more of them. Mr. Moffat, a pleasure. Miss Blackstock, your hat reminds me of springtime in the country, all these flowers bobbing happily. Almost makes me long for dead twigs."

Mr. Moffat watched him walk away with a perplexed look on his face. "He's an odd fellow."

Miss Blackstock nodded, then held her hand out to be helped up. "Yes, very odd. But also well-rounded, wouldn't you say?"

George St. Clair was intrigued. And he didn't like it one bit.

For seven days, he'd thought of only one thing.

One woman.

Two hats. Two smiles.

Countless barbs and insults delivered with bite. And a sweet hello delivered with none.

If he hadn't recognized her muddy brown eyes, he wouldn't have thought it the same woman.

Different hat, different mannerisms, different voice. Same woman.

He arrived early at the lecture hall the next week, then loitered outside until he felt like a fool and forced himself in.

He wondered who she would be bringing today, and when she finally came in the door, it was no one.

She met his eyes, then sat without a word.

He cleared his throat.

"Mr. St. Clair. You really should have that looked at."

"I see you're back to your twigs today. And alone, as well?" He looked around the room filled with men, and a handful of women, in somber-colored coats. "Do you think that wise?"

"I brought my maid again, she's just outside. Should I tell her to come in?"

He made a face. "No."

"It is unfortunate that I have tested and failed all of my acquaintances. I will simply have to hope that my honor is safe among steam enthusiasts." She shook her head. "I take my very life in my hands in this pursuit of knowledge."

His lips twitched. "We are a rowdy bunch."

She nodded in total agreement with him and he leaned forward in his seat to say quietly, "Does your Mr. Whoever know he is marrying a woman who wears two hats?"

"Mr. Moffat. And you must not know very many women if you think my two hats is at all remarkable."

"I've known more than a few. And none have had different smiles and different voices underneath those different hats."

She paused and George could practically hear the gears turning as she tried to come up with a response. She finally said, "A woman's hat is a reflection of her mood. When I am with my fiancé, I am happy. When I am here, I am. . . I. . . wish to be left alone."

He sat back in his seat. He opened his leaflet.

She turned to glare at him underneath *this* hat.

"It's only a twig."

"And when your Mr. Moffat was here, it was flowers and a bird's nest."

"I do not dictate fashion, Mr. St. Clair, but am merely a slave to it."

"Quite the slave. Your entire personality changes with it."

He leaned forward in his seat again and her eyes widened, not with wariness but with outrage.

He murmured, "Tell me it's nice to meet me while you're wearing this hat."

"So. Good. To. Finally. Meet. You."

He smiled. "So good to finally meet you as well, Miss Blackstock. Oh look, the lecture is about to begin."

Two

George didn't stop smiling, not for a long while.

Not when the lecture ended and Miss Blackstock leapt from her seat and stuck her nose in the air and walked determinedly away from him without another word.

Not when he arrived home to find a letter from his father and cheerily tossed it in the fire without reading.

Should have done that with Sinclair's letter as well.

He had the vague impression that some people enjoyed receiving correspondences but George did not. No good news ever came in one.

He sat down with one of his cigars, closing his eyes to imagine mud-colored eyes.

Engaged mud-colored eyes.

Poor fellow. He was in for a rude awakening on the wedding night.

Or perhaps Miss Blackstock would keep her happy hat on during the honeymoon phase. But one morning, Mr. Moffat would find himself peering underneath that twig hat wondering what had happened to the woman he'd married.

Honora Kempe fumed for seven days.

Miss Letitia Blackstock was asked multiple times over the course of the week if she was quite well. She snapped at her intended and insulted anyone who got near her, and Honora eventually quarantined herself.

And then she was forced to suffer her aunt and uncle tiptoeing around and whispering in hallways.

Honora squeezed her fist and shouted, "I can hear you!"

They poked their heads around the corner and Aunt Gertrude said softly, "The stress has got to you, my dear. Perhaps it was too soon to jump into the fray again. We should have waited, given you time to rest."

"It is too late now. We shall simply have to wait until Mr. Moffat decides he has had enough and pays us off."

Uncle Hubert muttered, "Shouldn't be too long now."

Aunt Gertrude patted her husband's arm. "Is that your plan then? To use this ill temper to force his hand?"

It hadn't been her plan. She hadn't had a plan, yet.

But she'd had five engagements broken and had never floundered for a reason for ending it yet.

Gentlemen, or at least those who thought of themselves as gentlemen, were willing to preserve the illusion of honor at any cost.

Uncle Hubert noted, "He hasn't been round in two days. You've scared him off."

"I told him I was not feeling well and I would send a note when I was better."

Her aunt and uncle exchanged a look, then came all the

way into the room.

Honora sat down and traced the pattern of the sofa with her thumb, and her aunt sat next to her.

"It might be for the best, dear, if you never sent that note. End this one, and we'll go have a rest. Be ourselves for a little while."

"It's too soon to end it. We've only been engaged for a month. We'll just have to use this *foul temper* to our advantage. Miss Letitia Blackstock will be her old happy self again tomorrow, and then in another month, I'll let Honora out and we can end this charade for good."

Another month of being Miss Letitia Blackstock, and Honora could feel her temper bubbling and boiling.

Perhaps her aunt was right and they'd rushed into this one. Honora couldn't explain why this persona chafed so but Miss Blackstock was getting on her last nerve.

She stood restlessly. "I am going to my lecture."

"Shall I go with you, my dear?" And when Honora shook her head, her aunt continued, "I don't know why steam interests you so."

Miss Blackstock would have explained, again.

But Honora simply said, "I know," and left the room.

Honora was late to the lecture– a carriage had overturned, blocking the road– and when she finally left her maid to wait outside the hall and quietly tiptoe inside, her temper and frustration gnawing at her, someone was sitting in her seat.

She stopped and glared at the offending gentleman.

Mr. St. Clair shifted in his seat and tried not to smile, and Honora turned her glare to *him*.

His eyes tipped up to look at her, yes, twig hat, and then he moved his walking stick from off the seat next to him and turned his attention back to the lecture.

Honora sat. And when Mr. St. Clair held out his leaflet to her, she took it without a word.

Mr. St. Clair leaned toward her and whispered, "Your hat is quivering."

Honora took a calming breath, opening the leaflet and willing her temper away. And then she laughed softly because she was sitting next to Mr. St. Clair and her temper wouldn't be improved with the experience.

But he said not another word and neither did she, and when the lecturer left the podium at the end, Honora was herself again.

Or as close to it as she could get while not actually being herself.

Mr. St. Clair held his hand out to Honora and she stared at it. "Er, yes?"

"The leaflet."

"Ah. Thank you for the use of it."

"You may be able to get another if you ask nicely." He glanced at her hat. "Or perhaps not."

She turned her head to look at him and his eyes were close. And gray. And amused.

"If I was wearing my other hat, I could probably get yours from you."

"I doubt it."

She did, too. But, "You simply can't imagine how men fall for a few flowers."

"Mm-hm."

He folded the paper, putting it inside his coat, and Honora asked, "Did you save this seat for me?"

"I didn't. But when I saw you getting ready to attack the poor gentleman who'd unwittingly sat in your favored spot, I decided I would rather hear the lecture. You were already causing a commotion by being late."

She smiled slightly. "A carriage overturned. You can hardly fault me for that."

"I can. I did. I will."

She rose and he followed her as she headed to the exit.

"Next week, I trust, I will be able to hear the entire lecture. A man should be able to expect that at least once."

"You've already had your once. Last week."

"Then once more, if you please, Miss Twiggy Blackstock. Next week is the final lecture."

Honora reared back. "Twiggy?"

"Your alternate ego is Miss Apple Blossom Blackstock."

She laughed, shaking her head as they exited the hall together. She spotted her maid and waved her over, and said, "Should I wear the other hat next week?"

"I can't imagine why you would."

He turned away from her after a quick head nod and Honora said to his retreating back, "No, I can't imagine why either."

Reparations were in order for Mr. Moffat, and Honora was forced to do what women had been doing since time immemorial.

She baked him a tart.

Of course, she burnt it, and she thought that if Mr. Moffat didn't get scared off because of her temper, her cooking might just do it.

Mr. Moffat's wife would have to know how to cook, at

least occasionally, and Honora was convinced that that was one skill that needed to be learned while young or else it just never took.

She'd thought about bribing Aunt Gertrude's cook to make a tart, then decided the truth might be better after all.

She packed a picnic basket and invited Mr. Moffat and Uncle Hubert and Aunt Gertrude and put on her Miss Apple Blossom hat.

They trudged through Victoria Park and when she found a suitable place, bade Mr. Moffat to lay down the blanket in as sweet a voice as she could muster.

It must have been good enough because Mr. Moffat smiled at her and they settled, Honora pulling out bread and boiled chicken and lemonade.

She waited until they had lunched, and then with a flourish pulled out her burnt strawberry tart with a bright smile.

She cut it up, placing it carefully on little plates, and when she passed Mr. Moffat his, said shyly, "A sweet treat to make up for my sour temper. Forgive me?"

Mr. Moffat said, "Of course, of course," as he looked at the tart with a frozen smile on his face.

Honora took a big bite of her own and said with obvious satisfaction, "Why, I think this is the best tart I've ever made. I remembered the sugar this time!"

Uncle Hubert choked and Miss Blackstock, ever solicitous, poured him more lemonade.

Aunt Gertrude got into the spirit of it and said, "You do not make the same mistake twice, Letitia, at the very least. This tart is a vast improvement, although a tad on the overdone side."

"Well, only a little. But I like my tarts well done. Don't you, Mr. Moffat?"

Mr. Moffat rapped his fork on the crust and finally said, "Er, yes. Wonderful, wonderful."

The next week, having learned her lesson about carriages and traffic, Honora was early to the lecture. And when she sat down, it was next to Mr. St. Clair again.

He looked at her. "You're not getting attached to me, are you?"

"I'm engaged."

He grunted. "Engaged is not married."

Honora thought no truer words had ever been spoken.

She said, "But you were relieved when I brought Mr. Moffat, weren't you?"

"Astounded was more like it. There should be some form of address for engaged women so as to warn a fellow. Not a miss, not yet a missus, but something in between."

"That is absurd. And unfair. You were born a mister, and there you'll stay. Whereas my very name, my very being, is dependent on whether I'm married or not."

"It's not about being fair, it's about keeping civilization going. A man needs to know if a woman is taken when he first meets her or else all hell would break loose."

"You're joking."

"No. A man needs to know at the first introduction so he stays away from another man's territory. A woman doesn't."

Honora realized her mouth was hanging open and she closed it with a snap.

"What you're saying is that a woman's form of address

is there simply to let a man know whether she is available or not? Fascinating."

He shrugged. "If your fiancé hadn't introduced us, you would have worked it in somehow that you were engaged. Isn't a form of address so much simpler?"

"I do believe I could have made it clear that I wasn't a possibility for you without resorting to my fiancé. But you are right about one thing. A woman doesn't need a man's form of address to tell her whether he's married or not. You're not."

"You don't know that. I could be married with four children and you wouldn't ever know."

"I know. You're not. And I think it unlikely you ever will be."

"Would that I was so lucky."

The lecturer took his place behind the podium and Mr. St. Clair leaned over to whisper, "Because I think that your Mr. Moffat, like all men, is in for a world of trouble once he says 'I do'."

Honora thought that if she really was going to marry Mr. Moffat, that was probably true.

Mr. Moffat looked, last time Honora had seen him, like he was beginning to realize that as well.

But it was going to take more than burnt tart and a bad temper to get him to break the engagement.

Honor. *Bah.*

Honora pushed every problem from her mind and listened as the lecturer waxed eloquently about what steam might bring them. Faster trains and ships. More goods and foreign foods from halfway around the world.

The impossible not only possible but already happening.

She glanced at Mr. St. Clair and knew that he saw it, too. The future.

She smiled at the curmudgeon, then turned back to the lecturer and imagined what steam would bring them.

When the lecturer stepped down from the podium and the audience had stopped clapping, Honora sighed.

"I will miss these lectures. You notwithstanding."

Mr. St. Clair gathered his walking stick. "Why? What is it about steam and coal and ships that grabs your attention?"

"I don't care whatsoever about steam or coal or ships."

"Then why do you come every week? Simply to torture me, I can only infer."

"It does have its perks. I do so enjoy the sound of a man clearing his throat at me. Have you had that looked at yet?"

He raised his eyebrows at her, not saying a word, and she said, "It's the future, isn't it? Speed and power and change. I care about the future. I care about paying for the future."

He turned fully in his seat to face her. "Of all the things I imagined you saying, that wasn't it. You care about paying for the future? Surely Mr. Moffat will take care of that for you."

Honora studied the leaflet in her hands. "My interest in paying for the future is no indication of Mr. Moffat's ability to provide."

"Do you think *he* will take it that way?"

"Are you giving me marriage advice, Mr. St. Clair?"

"Someone has to if you think you can invest without your husband's interference."

"Mr. Moffat did not seem too interested in steam."

". . .No."

"It's the future."

"Well, yes, but–"

"You think I should leave it to him. Because he's a man."

"I have never known any woman to have an interest in money beyond where to spend it."

"We have already established that you must not know that many women."

"I know absolutely zero women like you. I would have guessed that you insist on coming every week to interrupt my enjoyment."

"I didn't interrupt you today."

"No. But it is the seventh week and only the second time you haven't. I might be forgiven for my hyperbole."

"Perhaps you might be forgiven. If I was wearing a different hat."

"An impasse, then. I won't forgive you; you won't forgive me."

"However will we live with ourselves?"

"Lesser men would crumble under the weight."

"But not us."

He was silent a long moment, then finally his lips tilted northward and he dipped his head toward her.

"Not us, Miss Twiggy Blackstock. I assume you will be coming to enjoy the next lecture series as well."

She cocked her head. "I wasn't. What is it about?"

"Trains. Steam trains, specifically."

"Hmm. Perhaps I will."

He stood, waiting for her to rise, then followed until she met up with her maid.

He bowed. "Perhaps I will save you a seat."

Miss Twiggy Blackstock adjusted her hat and said, "Perhaps *I* will save one for *you*."

There was another letter waiting for George when he arrived home and he tracked down his valet to thrust it at him.

"I told you to refuse the post."

"Yes, sir. It is from your father."

"Yes. I specifically do not want any correspondence from him. I specifically do not want any correspondence from anyone."

"Yes, sir. Should I read it for you?"

George crumpled the letter and found the nearest fire. "Collin, if you looked any less like your sister, I would throttle you."

"If I looked any less like my sister, you wouldn't have hired me as your valet when I hid in your carriage."

"I should send you back home."

"Five years later? The threat has grown old, sir."

It had. He should have sent the boy back home when he was still a boy and not a man. Should have sent him home before he'd got his first glimpse of a London woman. Should have sent him home before London had shown him all that was missing in the country.

George stared at the fire and not into good, kind eyes. "Any news from home?"

". . .Another girl. They've named her Winifred."

"And your brother?"

"Still a pompous prig. Sir."

George nodded. "No more correspondences."

Collin sighed. "Yes, sir."

George went to his club to smoke. And be bored.

He didn't know when life had lost its sparkle. Didn't know when everything he'd once found pleasure in had become dull.

He thought of the country and his home, and wished he could go back. Go back to his youth, go back to his family.

Go back and rewrite the past.

But that was all impossible and he had no interest in going back to what currently was.

So he smoked. And thought of absolutely nothing and talked to absolutely no one.

No one hailed him, no one came over to bother him, not now that Sinclair was off to India again.

George was happy that no one bothered him.

Happy.

But he thought of muddy eyes that liked to spar with him. That liked to irritate him, and he thought she must like to irritate everyone. Liked to poke and rile when civilized men and women knew how to keep the peace.

And then he remembered her alter ego, Miss Apple Blossom, and thought she must know how to keep the peace as well.

Must know how to be sweet and womanly, she just didn't like to.

George puffed and smiled, forgetting that he was bored and lonely and instead imagined again the surprise Mr. Moffat would wake up to on his wedding day.

The harpy *had* saved a seat for him the next week and

when she picked up her leaflet to make room for him, he said, "This is perilously close to indecent, Miss Twiggy. What would Mr. Moffat say?"

She cocked her head and really thought about it.

"Do you think he would be worried that you were poaching on his territory?"

"If I was Mr. Moffat, I would be worried."

"You men are so very strange." She looked at him out of the corner of her eye. "Are you poaching?"

"You were the one who saved me a seat. If anyone is poaching, it is you."

"Oh, good. Because I'm not, you may rest assured. Now, if you were engaged, it might be poaching but in your case I think the correct term would be hunting."

He coughed. "Are you *hunting* me?"

"No, I was just pointing out the correct term. I'm engaged, Mr. St. Clair, please try to remember."

"If you acted like you were engaged, I might be able to."

She shifted in her seat to study him. "Would you be worth hunting? Are women lined up trying to catch you?"

"No."

"Not the eldest son of so-and-so?"

"No."

She faced forward again. "Ah, well. Better luck for the future."

"I have two older brothers. And a twin."

"Good God, there are three more of you? Your poor mother."

"Dead."

"Oh. Yes. Mine, too."

He nodded and they said not another word. No

condolences, not when they both knew condolences were worthless.

She rustled her leaflet and finally asked, "Three brothers. Any sisters?"

"I was spared. You?"

She fought a smile. "If half-sisters counted, I would have three."

"You don't like them?"

"I'm sure they are wonderful people now that they are out of leading strings. I haven't seen them in a long time, and stop me if you've heard this story before. Mother dies, Father remarries, new mother insists on breeding repeatedly so eldest daughter goes to live with her mother's sister."

He nodded. "The story is as old as time itself. I assume your aunt then treats you very poorly."

"Oh, no. She, and my uncle, spoil me rotten."

"That was my second guess."

"They weren't able to have children, you see. So they didn't realize that I was a handful."

His laugh surprised him. "How could they have missed it?"

The next week, he got there first and she huffed when she saw him already seated.

"You are too early. I'll have to leave the night before to get here before you."

"You must have quite the distance to travel. Your sacrifice for the future is impressive."

"No one cares more for my future than I do."

"You have a fiancé, and an uncle who spoils you rotten.

My guess is that there is a line of people who care for your future at least as much as you do."

Honora opened her mouth for a scathing retort, and then closed it. Because how could one softly spoken truth make her stomach clench with anger and shame? How could it make her feel ungrateful?

A long moment passed as they sat in silence and when her emotions were back under control, she said, "My fiancé and my uncle are both fine and wonderful men, but they don't have that need, that drive, to want more."

"And your father?"

"My father is too busy with his new family. If it was up to him, he would leave my mother's portion in her majesty's service for a measly five percent."

"Many widows and orphans live on that measly five percent."

"I know. I don't want to be one of them. And perhaps you're right. There *is* a line of men who care for my future; they just see it differently than I do."

"Ah, well, that is different then. And something I have experience with myself."

She remained quiet and met his eyes, and he said off-handedly, "My father."

"All fathers, I suspect. Did he want you to go into the military?"

"No. I did exactly what he wanted."

"Since there are few paths for a younger son from a fine family, I think you've trained to be a man of the cloth," she said and his eyebrows flew up in surprise.

He looked at her. *Looked* at her and *saw* her and Honora's heart raced.

She said, "Only those who've trained for it can invoke

guilt, shame, and ingratitude with a single phrase. Only those certain of their place in God's kingdom can be so condescending and self-righteous. The rest of us muddle along the best we can."

"Is this you muddling along?"

She held up her leaflet. "No. This is me studying."

This time it was he who fumed silently in his seat and she didn't let him get his emotions back under control.

She said, "I'm right, aren't I?"

"You've already decreed it. I doubt anyone dares contradict you."

"I have no doubt you would contradict me with great pleasure if you could."

"You know, Miss Twiggy. Though I barely met the man, I find I have great sympathy for your poor Mr. Moffat."

She said, "*Behold, we count them happy which endure*, Mr. St. Clair. James 5:11."

Three

George did not stay long after the lecture to argue with Miss Twiggy.

He kept hearing her confident tone declaring him to be a man of the cloth as if it was written on the lines of his face, the timbre of his voice.

I have no doubt you would contradict me with great pleasure if you could, and damned if she wasn't right.

He was a man of science. Of the future. Not a man forced to believe and parrot what was written down in a book centuries ago.

And yet, he was.

Or should have been.

But he'd returned home from university to find that his sickly twin had been nursed for the last few months by the love of George's life. That she was, instead of waiting for George, quietly engaged to his brother.

His father had sat him down. "It is a good match for everyone, George."

And George had told his father, shock still making his voice weak, "But I love her. And she loves me. I am sure of it."

"Perhaps. But she loves Henry as well. She is a sweet, country girl with no ambition and Henry will stay here, a country gent, and they will have a small, quiet, contented life."

George had whispered, "Father."

"Go to London," his father had said. "Enjoy yourself for a little while now that you're done with school. When the right living becomes available, I'll send for you."

George hadn't gone. He'd cornered Alice and begged her to run away with him.

And she'd patted his cheek and looked at George with good, kind eyes. "You will always hold a place in my heart, George. But I love Henry."

Then, George had gone after his brother.

Henry had been born thirty minutes earlier making him the older and George the baby of the family– but it had always been the other way around. Henry had always been weak and sickly, had always been babied and protected. Had always been loved, by everyone.

George had locked eyes with him. "You knew. You knew I loved her."

"I knew."

"And you asked for her anyway?"

"I loved her, too. You just never saw it."

George had stayed for the wedding, he didn't know why. Except maybe he had to see with his own eyes.

Had to see because he couldn't simply believe.

Had stayed, hoping to see regret in either of their eyes, but all he saw was happiness. And a love that should have been his.

He'd finally left when Alice had started feeling ill in the mornings. Gone to London just like his father had suggested and then had refused every living offered him since.

Even George agreed that his father had been patient beyond words. Five long years of support until that very afternoon when his banker welcomed him into his office and said, "Your allowance has been cut off."

George nodded.

Good show, Father. Good show.

George trudged home and when he arrived, Collin was polishing boots.

George watched for a long moment and then sat.

"Very well, tell me what was in the letters."

"Sir?"

"I know you opened them. Any self-respecting valet would."

Collin continued to polish.

George said, "I assume you knew my funds were to be cut off."

Collin sighed. "He did it?"

George nodded, closing his eyes and leaning his head back. "He did it."

"All is not lost, sir. He's found a living for you."

"Oh, God."

"Manchester."

George said again, "Oh, God."

"Yes, sir."

George decided he didn't need to open his eyes ever

again. He felt as if the very marrow had been sucked from his bones.

"When?"

"He wants you to come home first."

"He would."

"I have. . .appropriated. . .some funds for the trip," Collin said and George nearly smiled.

"You would."

"Shall I begin packing?"

George said, "Oh, God."

Mr. Moffat was finally getting a bit nervous about his fiancé's continued interest in steam lectures and kept trying to talk her out of going. When that proved impossible, he asked, "Shall I accompany you this week?"

"No! Of course not. You were bored silly last time."

"I worry about you. Flitting about all by yourself."

"I have my maid. And really, Mr. Moffat, I go straight to the lecture hall and then straight back. You saw the kind of people steam interests. It is not a fearsome bunch."

"But there were hardly any women present. I'm not sure it's seemly for you to go."

Mr. Moffat loved that word and Honora had to duck her face for a moment before answering.

"What is unseemly about education? And anyway, no one cares that I am a woman. No one has ever bothered me."

"What about that man who talked to you?"

"You mean Mr. St. Clair? There is no need to worry. He is as sour as always; I think it a permanent affliction."

Mr. Moffat said astutely, "Nothing goes better with

lemons than sugar."

Miss Blackstock simpered and tinkled a little laugh. "Mr. Moffat, you are so poetic. But there are many things sugar goes with. Strawberries, cherries. Oh! Shall I make you another tart when I get back from my lecture?"

She arrived nearly half an hour early for the lecture but before she could enter the hall and make sure she had bested Mr. St. Clair, a youngish boy tugged at her dress with his filthy hands and said, "Miss Twiggy?"

Honora stopped, preparing herself to fight him off and saying cautiously, "Yes?"

"Here." He thrust a folded up piece of paper at her. "The cove said you'd give me something for it."

She took it, unfolding it to read the name signed evenly and perfectly legible at the bottom, and her heart thumped.

She folded it back up quickly and dug in her reticule for a coin.

"I'm sure the cove gave you something already but thank you for keeping it clean."

He snatched the coin out of her hand and ran off, and Honora went inside the lecture hall. She took a leaflet and when she was settled and she couldn't take one more minute of imagining what George St. Clair could possibly write to her about, she unfolded the letter and placed it inside her leaflet to read surreptitiously.

One minute later, the excitement had been replaced with something else.

Not dread. How could she dread Mr. St. Clair leaving? He was nothing to her except an entertaining interlude.

Not anger. He wasn't foiling any plan of hers.

Perhaps disappointment.

Regret?

She looked at his even handwriting and knew Mr. St. Clair had felt the same something that she did.

A single gentleman sending a note to an engaged woman was perilously close to indecent and their relationship, if it could even be called that, did not require him to inform her of his imminent departure from London.

For good. For ever.

She stared at the podium. Then down at her leaflet.

Steam. Trains. The future.

Her future.

Honora Kempe got up quietly and left the lecture hall.

It took two weeks to get rid of Mr. Moffat.

A few temper tantrums.

A couple dinners, handmade.

Honora thought it most likely that her blackened toast and the resulting tantrum when Mr. Moffat could not get his teeth through it had been the final straw but eventually Mr. Moffat could take the thought of his future no longer.

Honora had sobbed and screamed and hysterically shouted how she was ruined and generally made Mr. Moffat absolutely sure that he was willing to pay any price to get rid of her.

And when Uncle Hubert stepped in with his quiet voice and calm acceptance, Honora had collapsed onto the sofa and cried into her handkerchief.

She cried and cried, never hearing the negotiation. Cried for herself, cried for poor Mr. Moffat and the five gentleman who had preceded him. Cried for her aunt and uncle.

Cried for her mother, gone so long ago.

Cried for the home she missed.

Cried knowing this game was all she would ever have.

Honora cried until she was all cried out.

She took a few shaky breaths and when she heard nothing, slowly lifted her head to find her uncle alone, his eyes closed. Just here in the room with her.

Honora's eyes prickled again and she blinked them back. She wouldn't cry because she *wasn't* alone. Wouldn't cry because her aunt and uncle, for some reason, had taken her in and loved her when no one else would.

Uncle Hubert asked, "Feeling better?"

She nodded though he couldn't see it and patted her sore eyes. "I do so hate Miss Blackstock."

"She is indeed very volatile," he said and Honora's laugh was wet and watery.

She wiped her nose on her soaked handkerchief and pushed herself into a more upright position.

"I believe it would do us all good to take a little break, Honora. Be ourselves for a while. With Mr. Moffat's donations, we have enough for a small cottage in the country. Enough for bread and cheese and the occasional joint of meat."

They had enough. Just enough. The word reminded her every time of what had been stolen from her and she said, "Letitia."

Uncle Hubert opened his eyes. "Still?"

"Still. I know where we're going next, uncle. I've found our Earl of Ferrers."

George St. Clair walked home.

The coach from the rail station had dropped him and Collin off at the village inn and despite Collin's wish to stop at the tap room for a refreshing and fortifying drink, George had merely picked up a bag in one hand and a side of his travel trunk in the other and waited.

Collin grabbed the other side sullenly and muttered, "The lord's son slinking home with his bags in his hand."

"The prodigal son. Everyone will enjoy the story."

"I want it to be known that I am not slinking home. I am merely following my employer."

"You're not going home at all. You'll be staying with me at the hall."

Collin blew out a breath. "Downstairs. And my sister up."

"That is awkward. Would you prefer to stay with your brother?"

Collin made a rude gesture and George laughed. "Funny how going home always brings out the child in each of us."

"Hilarious."

"I am sorry, Collin. I'm afraid I only thought how awkward this would be for me."

"You're a lord's son, sir. Selfishness is expected."

"You would think a lord's son could have trained his valet better."

"It is a complicated situation. But I will blame it all on Alice. Complicated awkwardness is unavoidable when someone marries above their station. I think your father was right to push Alice toward marrying Henry instead of you."

George stopped, his hand tightening around the handle of the trunk, and Collin stopped beside him to quietly say,

"Henry was always going to stay here. Her low parentage only makes it awkward for us, for family. But when you take your living, when you start moving up the church hierarchy as your father has always planned for you to do? Her birth and station would have been awkward for everyone."

"I should tell my father to take his living and his plans and give them to someone who wants them."

"Are you going to?"

"It does not seem likely."

Collin sniffed. "Manchester, then. And will you need a valet when you take your position or should I find my way back to London before I run into my brother?"

"Collin, who else is going to mouth off while dressing me if not you?"

"You have a point, sir. Now, should we go meet our nieces and nephew?"

Collin started walking again without waiting for a reply and George followed wordlessly, thinking selfish thoughts like any lord's son would do.

They had only just been welcomed inside when Alice came running, and when she saw her brother, her eyes filled with tears and she covered her mouth with her hand.

"Oh, Collin. You became a man. You've been gone too long!"

She hugged him, squeezing tight, then fussed with his suit and his hair.

Collin blushed bright red and he hissed, "Alice! I'm working!"

She laughed and swatted at him and she turned to

George. "You too, brother. You have been gone too long."

Lord St. Clair came out from a room, saying, "I agree. Too long."

Collin tried to get out of line of sight of the viscount, unsuccessfully since Alice was still clinging to his arm, and George had to give his father credit. He welcomed Collin warmly, told Alice to take her brother in to the sitting room so she could visit with him, and turned to greet his son.

George nodded at Collin to go and then stared back at his father who said, "Glad you could come."

As if I had a choice, George thought.

And, *I'm not.*

But he'd only just accused Collin of being childish now that they were home so he said, "Yes. It has been a long time."

"Let's go into the library. Henry is resting right now and you can say hello to the children when they come down to say goodnight. I think Alice and her brother will be busy for quite a while, which leaves us to discuss your new position. I confess when I heard how close it was to home, I jumped on it. I wish all my sons could stay near at hand and close enough to visit more often than every five years."

George said, "Hard to do when one son is stationed in Africa."

"He's a good writer, though," Lord St. Clair said to the son who wasn't. "Been promoted to Major. Moving up."

His father sighed as he sat, satisfied with his second eldest son's progress. "And you've seen Alice. Already recovered from the newest; I expect there will be many more."

"The child is. . .healthy?"

Lord St. Clair nodded proudly. "Healthy and strong. Her lungs! You'll hear her."

George couldn't keep the bitterness from his voice. "It's all falling into line for you, isn't it, Father."

"I have always said that your mother gave me four sons for a reason. One, for my heir. Two, for the military. Three, for the church. And four, to stay at home and bless me with a multitude of grandchildren."

"It is lucky for you that three of your sons followed your plan to fruition."

"The fourth one will as well."

The fourth one said, "Why? Why would I?"

"What else are you going to do?"

George sunk into his seat and closed his eyes.

His father said softly, "I know you wanted her, son. But you didn't *need* her, not like Henry. Her health when Henry has none. His relations when hers are lacking."

"Father, I don't want to hear how you bred them."

"And if I did? Their children are healthy and strong and they have a far better future than they would have, had their parents married others."

George opened his eyes. "Am I the only one who sees this part of you? That you think you are God?"

His father got that satisfied look on his face. "That is because you are a man of the church. You've been trained to see God everywhere."

George's disgust turned to dread. The fourth son *was* falling into line as well.

"Yes. I see God everywhere, as you say," he said and tried not to roll his eyes. "Tell me about this living."

"It's on the outskirts of Manchester, in the newly created diocese." His father beamed with pride, as if he'd not only single-handedly created this opportunity for his son but also the textile factories that employed the ever-growing number of immigrants looking for work, the coal mined in nearby hills that powered the heavy machinery, and the railways that transported finished goods out to the world.

"The town is growing so quickly! Nearly two dozen churches have been built in the area since you left school and a dozen more are in the planning stage. Your living should be comfortable enough for a bachelor, though you won't be able to stay one for long now."

"Sounds. . ." Horrifying? Depressing?

"I'll be going with you."

Torturous.

"I don't need a chaperone, Father."

"I'm not going for you. I've ordered the house opened. I spend some time there every year, checking my investments. Might as well do it now. You may stay with me until you're settled, if you like."

"I assume my allowance will not be reinstated any time soon?"

"You assume correctly. Once you've picked a wife, the matter will be revisited. We need to attract the right kind of woman for you, the kind of woman who will be comfortable hosting archdeacons, bishops. . .the archbishop. You won't be able to find that on a vicar's salary."

The entire thing was horrifying, depressing, and torturous.

George said, "When are we leaving for Manchester?"

"Is a week too long for you to spend at home, to visit with the family you haven't set eyes on in five years?"

Yes, it was.

George stood. "I'll need to bathe before dinner. I'll go find Collin."

Collin unpacked while George bathed, putting clothing away with a running commentary.

"She's the exact same. I thought maybe your family would have put some polish on her, but no."

"My father doesn't need her polished."

Alice was warm and welcoming and her children would be just like her. Healthy just like her, and George closed his eyes. Hating that his father had been right; hating that George could see it.

Collin said, "She's happy."

"Good."

"She says Henry's health cycles but at the moment he is doing well."

"Good," George said again.

"After we're done here, I'm going to run up to the nursery, see the children. Do you want to come?"

George opened his mouth to say that the children would be coming to say goodnight before dinner and he would see them then.

And then he thought of seeing Henry and Alice's children for the first time with his father watching and said, "Yes. Yes, I do."

Two towheaded children greeted the men when they entered the nursery, shouting, "Uncle Collin! Uncle George! Mummy said you would come!"

And though Collin had seen the children as often as George, meaning never, the young man fell to his knees and hugged them both. "It looks like Mummy was right."

A soft-spoken voice behind them said, "Mummy is always right."

George turned, looking over his brother carefully as he sat in a plush chair near the fire. Noting the frailness that never went away thanks to the wasting sickness that had plagued him since birth. Noting that he looked happy beneath the frailty as he watched his children pull Collin here and then there, showing off their toys.

"You're looking well, Henry."

"Feeling well, George. You look tired."

Tired. Of life.

But he went to stand next to Henry's chair and tried not to sound more tired than his sick brother. "It was a long trip from London."

"I hope you'll stay to rest. Take walks with me in the morning and naps in the afternoon, and you'll be feeling yourself again in no time."

George didn't think so. He was pretty certain that what ailed him couldn't be fixed with walks and naps, but he nodded at the brother he hadn't seen in years.

"I would love to join you on your walks, though I might skip the naps."

Henry chuckled lightly. "I know it sounds childish, but Alice swears by them. And I must admit, I feel better when I am able to sleep for a bit partway through the day. Invigorates me enough to last through dinner, at least."

Henry watched the children and Collin play with one toy after another, and George remembered how his brother had always had to sit and watch others play.

Henry said, "Alice and Father will appreciate having company a sight more active in the evenings and we'd all love to hear about London. How long are you planning on staying?"

"A week. Then I'm off to finally start my life."

But it felt as if George's life was ending. As if he knew exactly what the future held in store for him.

And he didn't like it one bit.

But, indeed, what else was there?

Collin played toy soldiers with the children, dying exuberantly and making them squeal with laughter, and when all three of them finally tired of it, Collin pushed himself from the floor, remembering loudly that he was a grown man of twenty and while he would have liked to stay all day playing, he had dinner clothes to prepare.

George said, "Awkward, indeed," and Collin said over his shoulder as he closed the door behind him, "I'll remind you for Boxing Day."

Henry shot a disappointed look at George. "Boxing Day? He is family, George."

"As he points out every year, he is both family and a servant, and so deserves gifts on both Christmas *and* Boxing Day."

Henry laughed. "Ah. Very well then. I am glad you have someone, George, who is not afraid of you. I am glad you are not alone."

"Afraid of me? Are you?"

Henry thought for a long moment. "Not afraid, but you can be very severe. I'm glad Collin is there to poke at you."

"He does an admirable job of it."

"Perhaps once you're comfortable in your new living, you can add a wife to your small circle."

George sighed, and thought he might need a long nap every day after all.

"Father will no doubt find me a suitable wife who loves to poke at me as well as Collin."

"For an old widower, he does not do a bad job of picking out exactly what one needs."

The baby started her howling at that moment, the sound making George's ears tingle even through the closed door.

"How in the world can something so small be so loud?"

Henry smiled as if her screams were the sweetest sound he'd ever heard. "You should hear when she really gets going."

"Father did say she had some lungs on her."

Henry closed his eyes to listen to the life bellowing from his child, and George watched him, wondering how many of the seven deadly sins a man could break while looking at his brother.

A week was far too long to stay but he did.

And at the end of it, he hugged the children goodbye, kissed Alice's cheek like a brother, thumped Henry gently on the back as if they were good friends.

He didn't look back when the carriage began its journey to Manchester.

Lord St. Clair sat across from him and said, "I was right about them, wasn't I?"

"Yes, Father."

The older man nodded. "I'll be right about you, as well. You'll see."

Manchester

Sinclair,

Glad to hear you have landed in India. The place must agree with you, or it is as I have always suspected and you are simply a lucky scoundrel. The widow has made an honest man of you and there is a child on the way? Just how long is the journey to the edge of the world?

All joking aside, I am very happy for you, old friend. Happy to have been wrong about that, and well wishes to the both of you.

Your friend, who will be joining you in matrimony fairly soon if Father has any say in the matter,

St. Clair

Four

Miss Letitia Blackstock had changed a little. Scandal will do that to a girl.

She smiled a little less. She wore her twiggy hat a little more.

Those who had known her in London, and there were a few unfortunately, noted the change. And whispered about it.

Aunt Gertrude stood at the edge of a smallish ballroom, watching those around them dance and laugh and include them not at all and said, "I didn't think any place could be worse than London. Perhaps it is the season."

Honora said, "It's the rain. It hasn't stopped since we got here."

Uncle Hubert cleared his throat. "It's rained no more than it did it London. It's the welcome."

It *was* the welcome. Or, rather, the unwelcome.

The few acquaintances who'd known her, or of her, had made short work of her ruined engagement. She was surprised they'd been invited to any gathering at all, and if she had still been Miss Apple Blossom Blackstock, she would have been grateful and thankful to be allowed here on the outskirts.

She wasn't Miss Apple Blossom Blackstock any longer, thank the Lord.

And Miss Twiggy wouldn't be grateful for small, poisonous favors.

She said, "I don't care a fig whether they welcome me or not. There is only one person I care to see and I want him to know that I am a free woman."

"But will he welcome you, my dear? Miss Blackstock has been tarnished."

"I must believe that he won't care, Aunt. The real problem is running into him. Our circles do not overlap."

"You mean his and Miss Blackstock's circles do not overlap."

That *was* what she meant. Honora Kempe might have been his equal but, "Since Miss Blackstock is how he knows me, that is who I must stay."

"I would say he must know you very little. Did the matter of who your father is come up at all?"

Honora tried to remember. Had she ever mentioned her father? And if so, what had she told him?

Lies were so easy to confuse.

"If we can but find him, I can figure out what I told him about my father. And embellish, should I need to."

"Perhaps Mr. St. Clair is not in Manchester."

Perhaps. His note had given her very little information. Only that he was leaving London for Manchester, and offering her and Mr. Moffat a hearty "good luck".

It had turned out to be harder than she'd expected to

find one man in a town that was rapidly approaching 300,000.

Honora said, "Then we are here, in this dreary and hostile land, for nothing."

Her aunt and uncle shared a glance over her head and Honora pretended not to see it.

Pretended not to see the conjecture in the men's eyes and the contempt in the women's.

It did not improve her mood to know that she deserved both, though not for the reason they assumed.

She *knew* she would not see the same in Mr. St. Clair's. . .

She *hoped* she would not.

She had not a clue how to find him though. He was indeed out of Miss Blackstock's circle and she could not go chasing after a man openly, not now. Could not ask about him, though she sent her uncle to try and find him.

Had she known that one day she would hunt Mr. St. Clair, she would have asked more direct questions of him.

"Letitia," her aunt began, and Honora shook her head.

She could hear the defeat in their voices. Could hear the exhaustion, could hear that at some point this game had stopped being fun.

"We only need one more and then we are done for good." Honora tipped her head up, resolved. "We'll stay here until we know of somewhere else to look."

Uncle Hubert said, "Just imagine, Gertrude. A small house on the edge of a small town. Enough money for warm rooms, fine clothes, good meat."

"Good ale, I suspect as well."

"If you must," he said and made both women laugh.

Honora slipped her arms through theirs, one on either

side of her. "Enough for books and the well wishes of our neighbors."

"He'll give that to us? All of it?"

"He will," Honora said. "I know he will."

If they could ever find the blasted man.

It was months before she did and she'd nearly given up on him.

Uncle Hubert and Aunt Gertrude had, and while they'd asked once if perhaps there wasn't another gentleman in Manchester that might work in his stead, Honora had refused.

One more man. One more engagement.

She would save it for him.

And then one day, she found him the exact same way she'd found him in the first place.

At a lecture on the wonders of steam boilers.

She stopped stock still and stared at him and blinked wildly, wondering if perhaps Manchester and it's rain and unwelcome society had made her go mad.

He rose and made his way to her, looking just as shocked as she, although perhaps less stupidly so.

"Why, Miss Twiggy. Or should I say Mrs. Twiggy?"

Honora opened her mouth and blinked some more.

"Miss Blackstock? Er, Mrs. Moffat? I now quite understand how irritating one could find a name change."

Honora closed her mouth and stopped her incessant blinking and said scintillatingly, "Yes. Quite annoying."

"It is. Yes."

". . .It is Miss Blackstock still."

"Ah. And here I was imagining running into Mr. Moffat

and seeing what wedded bliss had turned him into."

He offered her the seat next to him and she sat wordlessly.

Just how, she wondered blankly, was one supposed to bring up the fact that Mr. Moffat was no longer?

She'd thought, months ago, that she could simply laugh and say he met Miss Twiggy and called off the wedding. But it had been too long, now.

After a long awkward moment, she simply said, "I'm sorry, Mr. St. Clair. You've surprised my wits away."

"I have no doubt they will return with force, Miss Blackstock."

"I do hope so," she said with an embarrassing wobble.

She looked down at her leaflet, sitting next to him once again, and nearly cried out, *I thought I had lost you. I thought I had missed my chance. And here you are.*

He said, "Now, what are you doing in Manchester? Has it become fashionable?"

"Nooo."

He chuckled. "I am relieved. I'm not sure I want to live in a world where Manchester is the place to go to be seen."

The speaker began to make his way to the podium and Honora leaned toward Mr. St. Clair. She said softly, "Do you remember you said that if you'd never met Mr. Moffat, I would have still worked him into the conversation? To warn you that I was taken and off-limits."

"I remember. You seemed to be quite insulted by the idea."

"I think you were right. It would be so much simpler if there was a form of address for a woman who used to be engaged, but now is no longer."

This time, it was he who sat there looking stupid and

awkward and uncomfortable.

"Did he. . .pass?"

"No," she said. "He met Miss Twiggy."

Mr. St. Clair sucked in a breath and said softly, "Before the wedding." And then, sharply, "He called it off?"

She nodded.

"A cad, I thought so from the very beginning. I am sorry, Miss Blackstock."

Honora's wits, at last, returned and she stuck her nose in the air to haughtily say, "I'm not."

Honora did not go straight home. She couldn't.

She simply couldn't.

So she walked, her maid trailing farther and farther behind and unable to see the tears streaming down her mistress's face.

It was the weather. It was Manchester. It was being unwelcome and unliked and *pitied.*

There was nothing worse than being pitied by those you yourself pitied. Those who were silly and blind and stupid.

Except, it was worse being pitied by someone you very nearly liked. Someone who, if one wasn't going to swindle a nice and comfortable living from, one would actually enjoy being around. Someone who wasn't silly or stupid, though probably still blind.

He had to be. He *would* be.

He would be worth the last few horrid months. He would be worth being Miss Letitia Blackstock for a little while longer.

And then, when it was over, when they were assured a warm and well-fed and free future, she would finally let

Miss Honora Kempe out again.

And try and remember just who she was.

St. Clair smiled on the way home, remembering Miss Twiggy's *I'm not.*

He stopped smiling when he remembered her shocked face and defeated posture when she'd first seen him. How could any honorable gentleman do that to a woman and force her to Manchester of all places?

No wonder they'd left London. A broken engagement was a spinster sentence, and George could very well imagine why Miss Blackstock had been so shocked to see him. Especially when the first thing out of his mouth was to ask about Mr. Moffat.

How could he have known? He couldn't have.

But that didn't change the fact that he wished he had. That he wished he hadn't said anything and could have remembered her as the ferocious Miss Twiggy for always.

He hoped it would return. Hoped she would return, next week.

That stopped him and he paused before going inside. Surely, Miss Twiggy could not be scared away. Surely, Miss Twiggy was in there still.

Licking her wounds, perhaps. But still there.

He pushed in the door to his little home, calling for Collin before shrugging off his coat.

The vicarage suited him, he'd been surprised to find. A new home, next to a new church built to accommodate the growing population on the outskirts of town.

The congregation was welcoming but that might have only been because he was young and there was an overabundance of unmarried young women in the vicinity.

A woman came in to cook and clean during the week and George had thought that he might hire a dedicated cook but the need had never arisen. Collin could make tea and boil an egg if needed, but since baskets of meat pies, savory stews, and freshly baked bread invariably found their way to his doorstep with a note inviting him to dinner, it was rarely necessary.

The women wanted to make sure that the bachelor vicar remained robust, and not a bachelor for very much longer.

He tried not to abuse their hospitality but it was his duty to get to know the members of his parish. And, because he was a man with limited experience in fawning women, he did enjoy a few dinners every week.

Collin came down the steep stairs lightly. "And how was the lecture?"

"You remember I told you about the steam woman in London?"

Collin paused. "Err, no."

"The one at the steam lectures with the poor fiancé."

"Oh, yes. The abrasive one."

"She's here! She was at the lecture. And *sans* the fiancé; a free woman, as it were."

Collin resumed his descent, going straight to the coat George had just hung up to brush the dust from it. "That is a very strange coincidence that she turned up here, in Manchester."

"Very strange. She nearly fell over in shock when she saw me."

"And yet, still managed to let you know the fiancé was no more."

"I did ask about him quite pointedly."

"Hmm."

"What?"

Collin pulled papers from the coat pockets and sorted through them. "Just, hmm."

"She suffered a change of circumstance and wanted a fresh start."

"And she chose Manchester." Collin pointedly looked at him. "You're the son of a lord. With a living. Need I remind you that you're a catch?"

George snorted and shook his head and went to sit before the fire for awhile. To warm his toes and remember. London and a woman who'd shocked him senseless. An engaged woman he'd been overly familiar with because she was safe.

Taken.

And now she wasn't.

He remembered a woman who had looked at him with a spark in her eye and said, *In your case, I think the correct term would be hunting.*

The next week he was late to the lecture and he'd rushed in to find Miss Blackstock already seated with an empty spot beside her. George sat down with a brief nod and a curt, "Are you hunting me?"

Miss Blackstock glanced at him. "We've already had this conversation. Please try to keep up."

George tried not to find her amusing, really he tried. But she was. And he did.

"I see your wit has returned. Good for you. But during that conversation, you had a fiancé and now you don't."

"It's true. I did, and I don't. I. . .am not at all sure I would like to have another. You are safe with me, Mr. St. Clair."

The lecturer took his spot and began speaking, and George leaned close to whisper in her ear, "I'd like to believe you. I would."

She replied just as quietly, "And I am wondering why exactly you don't."

She moved, just a small shift, and her arm brushed his.

"Perhaps it's your choice of wordage. I am safe with you but am I safe *from* you?"

"There is a distinction, isn't there? Because I assume I am safe from you but *with* you. . . I should make my maid come in next time. She can sit between us."

"Sounds horrible. *I* assume this maid is as loud as the last one."

"It does seem like a reasonable assumption. Perhaps there is some assurance you can give me so we don't need to go down that path. Perhaps you became married since London? I can't tell by *your* address, and either I've become immune to your manners or else there is a woman working her magic behind the scenes."

George couldn't help his smile. "No wife. No fiancé. I can't even assure you that I am not looking for one, either. It is a truth universally acknowledged that a single man in possession of a good living must be in want of a wife, no matter his feelings on the matter."

She gasped, twisting to meet him eye to eye. "I knew it! I knew you'd trained for the cloth."

Her triumph was palpable and loud, even though it was still whispered, and a gentleman two rows in front turned around to scowl at them.

George stared into Miss Blackstock's eyes– brown, they were brown with green and gold flecks– and said, "You knew it because I am condescending and self-righteous."

"Yes. *Preach the word, be instant in season, out of season, reprove, rebuke, exhort. . .* 2 Timothy 4:2," she said, but there was a smile on her lips and a twinkle in her eye.

They lasted a long moment, facing each other and glorying in their own triumphs until Miss Blackstock pulled away from him. She sat back in her seat, turning her attention to the lecturer again and George watched, a twisty unfamiliar emotion swirling inside him.

Intrigue, perhaps.

Interest, definitely.

Because he wouldn't mind at all if she was hunting him.

"I know nothing about her!"

George threw the letter he'd just received toward the fire. He'd been expecting it and therefore had saved it from the now customary fiery fate– only to find that his solicitor could not find any information on Miss Letitia Blackstock.

To be fair, George had given the man very little information to work with. Her name. Her former fiancé's name. She lived with an aunt and uncle, and no George didn't know their names.

Blackstock, he would imagine. Unless the aunt was the blood relation.

Names were so very trying, he was beginning to realize.

Collin watched George pace back and forth, back and forth, and repeated mildly, "You know nothing about her."

He'd said that before, when he'd watched George pen his original letter to the solicitor, and George had replied,

"I know. I want to find out more. Thus, the letter."

"And why this sudden interest?"

"It's not sudden. I've been telling you about her since Lon–"

"Then why this suddenly serious interest?"

"She asked if I was married. Not in so many words, of course. And don't interrupt your employer."

Collin had waved away George's admonition with a satisfied nod. "She's chasing you."

"No. It's not a chase. There's a glimmer in her eye, there's a flush to her skin, there's a. . .brain. . .a will. . .a plan. It's something more than a chase. She's hunting me."

Collin's eyebrows had slammed together. "You sound positively happy about it."

George had smiled. "I am. Yes."

"And you know nothing about her."

George had stopped smiling and said a word no vicar should even know.

He said that word again, today, and then said, "I don't know nothing. I just don't know enough. Yet."

Collin ran a finger along the mantelpiece, checking the housemaid's work. "I think I would like to know a little bit more about Miss Blackstock. Perhaps I will join you today at the lecture."

"Because having one's valet accompany you to a lecture is not strange at all."

"Then perhaps I will go as your brother-in-law."

George paused in his pacing and cocked his head. "Slightly less strange for the general population. Slightly more strange for me."

Collin said, "That's decided then."

They had already arrived and found their seats before the thought occurred to George that this might have been a horrible idea.

"Collin, you will be quiet during the lecture. No chatting, no fidgeting, no snoring, no knitting."

Collin raised an eyebrow. "I'll do my best."

"This was a horrible idea. What was I thinking? If you interrupt the lecture, I will be forced to replace you."

"Try again, George. And try to remember that today I am your brother-in-law and not your valet."

"I did remember. And don't call me George."

"Of course not. Sir." Collin turned in his seat to get a better view of George and said, "Are you always so nervous to see her?"

"Nervous? I don't want you interrupting the lecture. It has nothing to do with her."

"Of course not. Sir."

Collin's eyes roamed toward the door and he jerked his chin at it. "Since I've only seen one other woman here and she must be older than my granny, this must be Miss Blackstock."

George turned in his seat to find Miss Twiggy heading right for them and he rose as she approached.

"Miss Blackstock, may I introduce Mr. Collin Clarke, my brother-in-law. . .so to speak. Our siblings are married. His sister, my brother."

"Mr. Clarke. Have you come to be entertained by the wonders of steam?"

"Not in the least," Collin said and George said over him, "I've taken him under my wing."

Miss Blackstock looked between them for a long minute, then sat and made herself comfortable.

When George and Collin had followed her example, she said, "He's not going to interrupt the lecture, is he?"

Collin nearly fell out of his seat laughing and George tried mightily to ignore him.

"I've already warned him off knitting," George said gruffly and when Miss Blackstock chuckled at his wit, he suddenly found it much easier to keep his attention focused on her.

George apologized for his brother-in-law's laughter. "He's young."

"Yes. Should we send him out with my maid?"

George and Collin walked home in companionable silence. George, because he had sat next to Miss Blackstock and whispered to her and been whispered at, and he didn't care what Collin thought. Not at that moment.

Perhaps he never would.

George realized Collin's silence was not quite as companionable when the young man sighed and said, "Why do you always fall for the most inappropriate woman? It's as if your heart won't even wake up to notice unless your father would hate her."

George blinked and suddenly felt the coolness of the night.

"What's inappropriate about her?"

"She's. . .outspoken."

George nodded. "So are you."

Collin snorted, then nodded his head in acquiescence. "True. Though not to your father and I suspect the same could not be said for Miss Blackstock."

George was glad for the darkness. Glad no one could see how he smiled at the thought of Miss Blackstock meeting his father.

"I suspect you are correct."

"And if that doesn't carry weight with you, I suspect she would also be outspoken with bishops, arch or otherwise."

George's smile grew a little meaner. "She would be quite unimpressed."

"Think, George, what that would mean for your career. Your future."

"You mean my father's hope for my career. This line of reasoning is not going to change my mind about her, you know?"

"I know. Because you're the lord's son and you think what you like."

George grinned, then nodded when Collin said, "She's a little long in the tooth."

There was something about the woman that proclaimed she had seen the world. There was a lack of naivete. Of wonder.

As if her innocence had left her long ago.

George shut that thought down quickly.

"She's not old. She's just not young. I would guess we are near the same age."

"Like I said, long in the tooth."

George said, "Perhaps you should ask her next time you meet just how old she is."

"It worked for her uncle's name, didn't it?"

"Yes."

It had. And neither of them had missed the attention she paid to the question.

Collin said, "There's something too aggressive about her."

"I think Miss Blackstock could handle any situation she found herself in. Father would like that."

"We know nothing about her, George."

"This is a very bad habit you're starting, with this name thing. And we have her uncle's name now. We'll just learn a little more about Miss Blackstock, won't we?"

Collin sighed. "Why couldn't you have fallen in love with the girl who made those hot cross buns?"

George stopped on the pavement. Fallen in love? Had he?

He'd only loved one woman before and the memory now was distorted. Corrupted by everything that had come after.

In love?

No. He didn't know enough about her. Not yet.

But for the first time, he thought he might be willing to fall again.

George started walking and when he came level with Collin, he patted his friend, brother, and valet on the back.

"I couldn't ever fall in love with the hot cross bun girl. I don't want a tubby valet."

Five

When Honora arrived the next week, there was Mr. St. Clair, alone, in their customary spot.

She sat down next to him without a word, he continuing to read his leaflet with great concentration, and Honora wondered how they could be here, surrounded by people, and yet it was just the two of them.

It had been illuminating to see him interacting last week with his brother-in-law, with someone he was obviously close to and fond of, and when he began to speak softly, she thought he sounded like he was still talking to a friend.

"How do we proceed, Miss Blackstock? I am lost."

Honora turned her head enough to see that he was still studying his leaflet.

"Perhaps there will be another lecture after this one, Mr. St. Clair. Steam is not likely, but perhaps. . .Egyptian antiquities? I admit I have no real fondness for mummies or the desert or long-dead languages. Still, I had no interest in steam before falling into my current fascination. There's hope."

"Is there? Another lecture and another because we did this all wrong?"

She smiled slightly at his profile. "We did, didn't we? No balls, no dancing, no chaperones."

"No context. I am supposed to be able to ask delicate questions to your relations and acquaintances, and you are supposed to be able to do the same to mine."

"I missed my chance. I should have asked your brother-in-law."

Mr. St. Clair sighed. "I never had the chance. Unless you count the time I physically accosted your uncle."

Honora blew out a breath before it turned into a much-too-loud laugh.

He said, "Or the time I verbally accosted your aunt. And your maid. And you. Bloody hell, I should just be happy I can sit next to you in a crowded lecture hall."

He turned his head toward her and he didn't have to say that he was. Happy to sit here with her, as happy as Honora was to sit here with him.

They sat together, alone in the crowded room, and she said, "I suppose I could bring my uncle to the next lecture."

George closed his eyes and Honora wanted to laugh again at his pained look.

Before he could agree to such a ridiculous suggestion, she said, "Or I could extend to you his invitation to dinner."

"His invitation or yours?"

"Both of ours."

He opened his eyes and raised an eyebrow at her.

Honora smiled. "My uncle is a good, kind man. Slow to

anger and quick to forgive. Besides, he was hardly awake when you assaulted him. He doesn't equate you with the gentlemen I've been. . ."

She stopped and looked down at her lap. Then decided to give him the truth. Because she'd begun this dance half a dozen times before and had never had a truth to give any of them.

". . .the gentleman I've been boring them with for the last few months."

When she looked back up, he was looking forward and smiling stupidly. He said softly, "You know nothing about me. And I know nothing about you."

"Nothing? Then you must be very unobservant because I know quite a bit about you."

His smile grew. "You're right, Miss Blackstock. It's not nothing."

Honora flew around their Manchester home, making sure everything was perfect for Mr. St. Clair.

Every pillow in its place. Every table setting just so.

She did not dare step foot in the kitchen, just in case her presence burned the meat or scalded the soup, and instead kept sending her aunt in to make sure everything looked good.

They'd spent days agonizing over what to serve for dinner.

"Something simple?" her aunt had asked.

"No. He's somebody. Somebody's son."

"He's a vicar. A bachelor vicar. I expect meat and potatoes and bread, and he'll be happy."

Honora made a face. "He's nothing like Mr. Moffat. He

won't be impressed by country fare, nor worried at all about whether his wife can cook. Do you think our cook could make turtle soup?"

Aunt Gertrude choked. "No. Not even if we could afford it."

Honora blew out a breath and tried to remember back to a different lifetime. She muttered to herself, "What would Father have served to a dignitary?" and Aunt Gertrude had nearly fallen out of her chair in shock at the mention of the man.

They'd finally settled on oxtail soup, roasted hare, stewed cardoons, pigeon compote, kidney beans, lamb's tongue with spinach, and almond cake.

A beautiful dinner, Honora told herself over and over again, trying to calm her abnormally nervous stomach while her maid curled her hair.

The girl looped and tugged and smoothed, and completely ignored the ornament Honora had told her to use.

"You're forgetting something."

"Please don't make me put it in your hair, miss. Look, I brought some baby's breath. It'll look lovely draped down your neck."

Honora said, "The twig," and her stomach settled.

Mr. St. Clair arrived right on time with his brother-in-law and when Honora introduced her uncle, she laughed.

"We really have gone about this in completely the wrong way."

Her uncle said, "The world is changing and quickly. My niece tells me all about steam and I am appalled at the speed of this new world."

"You're not appalled at what that speed brings, though. Oranges are his favorite treat."

Mr. St. Clair said, "Cigars are mine."

Uncle Hubert perked up. "Oh, do you smoke. . ."

And off they went into the land of ghastly manly pleasure, whence no woman could possibly want to follow.

Aunt Gertrude said, "They'll be awhile, I think. Do you smoke, Mr. Clarke?"

"Not at all. I can't stand what it does to a good coat."

Aunt Gertrude nodded. "Oh, I agree. Though hopefully, you like oranges?"

Mr. Clarke professed he did and they chatted about fruit while Honora wished she'd listened about having an even number of guests.

She'd fallen down in her duty as a hostess, purposefully– after all, who would they have invited?

And if they'd been familiar with any other families in Manchester, why would she want another female around her Mr. St. Clair?

Honora paused and looked at her Mr. St. Clair.

Hers. Hers?

Mr. Clarke caught her staring at his brother-in-law. "Forgive me, Miss Blackstock. I'm sure I can think of something more scintillating to talk about than fruit."

"Enjoy your conversation. Your turn will come soon enough when Mr. St. Clair and I bore everyone silly with our talk of water and coal and trains and ships."

Mr. Clarke and Aunt Gertrude closed their eyes in supplication but Mr. St. Clair heard her. He turned his head enough to meet her eyes and a slight smile hovered at the corners of his lips.

Honora's uncle continued to wax lovingly about cigars, and Mr. St. Clair continued to smile, and Honora tried to pay attention to her aunt and Mr. Clarke as they turned the conversation to London.

There was no agreement here. Mr. Clarke had loved every bit of it and her aunt felt the opposite.

"Now, York," she said, "is the finest city in all of England. A wall that surrounds and a minster that watches over. Have you been?"

He shook his head. "I've never been able to talk St. Clair into sightseeing at Brighton and Bath. Do you think I'd have better luck with York, Miss Blackstock?"

"Perhaps. Would he be tempted by ancient Roman artifacts? A ruined abbey? Richard III?"

As she listed all of York's ancient wonders, Mr. Clarke's shoulders slumped and when she finished he said, "No. Unless there is loud machinery and unpardonable speed, he won't care at all."

Aunt Gertrude shook her head. "What a shame. It's a lovely place. I hope we can return one day."

When she met Honora's shuttered eyes, she amended, "For a visit. I wouldn't mind taking a stroll atop the wall one more time."

Mr. St. Clair and Uncle Hubert had wandered over during the discussion and Uncle Hubert laid his hand gently on his wife's arm.

"It must be the memories and not the place, my dear. What could be so special about a wall?"

Honora looked away from their secret smiles. Away from all that they'd left behind in York.

People and places they'd never see again.

Memories.

The future.

Mr. St. Clair touched her elbow. "And do you feel the same about York, Miss Blackstock? I confess my one visit did not impress me."

"You've been to York?"

"A pilgrimage of sorts. My father wanted me to see the minster. And the ruined abbey. But I was young, and well, disagreeable, so perhaps that colored my visit."

"Disagreeable, Mr. St. Clair? I can hardly believe it of you."

Aunt Gertrude tsked. "Honora!"

But Mr. St. Clair looked at the decoration in her hair and then down into her eyes and even her aunt could see that he did not look at all disagreeable *now*.

Aunt Gertrude found something on the other side of the room for Mr. Clarke to look at posthaste and Mr. St. Clair murmured, "I'd have been truly worried if there were spring flowers in your hair and not a twig."

"No flowers for you, Mr. St. Clair. I fear you have always been privy to my true disposition and there is no use hiding it now. I am but an open book."

"Now that, I doubt. But you may try and prove it by telling me what you thought of York. You did not look as misty-eyed as your aunt and uncle during the discussion."

Honora inhaled a deep breath, then lied. "We lived there only for a short time. Right after my mother died. I hardly remember it."

"You are quite nomadic, Miss Blackstock. York, London, Manchester."

Bath, Edinburgh, Wales. It was easier to list the places they *hadn't* lived.

She said, "When one loses something important, Mr. St.

Clair, one will search the world for its replacement. Or, at least the entirety of the British Isles."

"Yes," he said, and his own loss was in his voice.

She knew he'd lost his mother, too. And was happy to let him think that's what she was speaking of.

He took her hand. "Have you found it yet?"

She looked down at his gloved hand cupping hers. She didn't dare look up; knew she couldn't keep her thoughts off her face as she whispered, "Have you?"

The gentlemen were pressed to come to dinner again the next week and neither one of them was reluctant to accept.

Collin waited until they were nearly home before offering his opinion. "I will not squirrel you away from her machinations just yet."

George could still feel her hand in his, could still see the twig in her hair, could still smell her scent.

He said, "Good. You would have a rough go of it."

"I could always write to your father."

George grunted.

"But it does seem mutual, this complete loss of reason, so. . .I'll hold off on that."

George murmured, "Excellent."

He was nervous as a school boy the day of the next lecture. Collin helped him into his coat and said, "Shall I come with you?"

"No."

"But who will keep you in line?" he asked, making George wonder how out of line Miss Blackstock would let him get.

Wondering if he should make her bring her maid inside today because the thought of sitting next to her without any kind of chaperone suddenly seemed ill-advised.

But then, she was right there next to him. And he couldn't remember why he wanted a chaperone. He couldn't remember anything except his own name.

He didn't even notice the silence until she said, "Well, this is awkward."

He jerked. "It is? I was simply enjoying your presence."

Her voice was quiet and warm when she replied, "Mr. St. Clair, you are simply ruining your reputation. I expect gruffness and irritability and a sour bite to all your declarations."

He said, "I detest how much I enjoy your company, Miss Blackstock. Is that better?"

"Yes. Quite perfect. And interestingly enough, exactly how I feel about the situation."

But it was a step too far, this mutual declaration and he adjusted his seat.

"Nothing may come of this. I want to warn you."

She nodded, still without looking at him. "I don't mind walking down this path with you a little further."

He smiled. "That is *exactly* what I am proposing."

"I will warn you, Mr. St. Clair. Something may come of it."

"Yes." He nodded. "Yes, something might. And since there is no one else to ask, I'll have to be gauche and direct."

"Oh, dear. However will I survive."

"About Mr. Moffat."

"Oh. . . Dear."

She opened the leaflet that had been sitting on her lap

and began to read. Or at least pretend to.

"A broken engagement, Miss Blackstock, is noteworthy."

She nodded her head once, sharply. She chewed on her top lip for a brief moment and then said briskly, "The truth is, Mr. St. Clair, that I didn't like who I had to be when I was with him. And I didn't realize until too late that perhaps I could simply be myself. I don't blame him for calling it off. He thought he was marrying a woman sweet and kind."

"I met her."

She smiled, then stopped. "Do you miss her?"

". . .I didn't know her well enough to miss her. And I doubt I would have noticed her at all if I had not met you first."

She finally turned her head to face him and he said, "I'm confusing myself. I know it was you, always."

She sounded infinitely sad as she said, "No. This is me."

"Miss Twiggy."

"Yes." She smiled tightly and leaned closer, staring into him with wide eyes and whispering, "There was no impropriety on either of our parts. I actually think. . . I think it was quite brave of him. He did something that I was unwilling do and it would have been much easier if I had been the one to call it off. He sacrificed his honor and saved us both from a very unhappy future."

"He was a scoundrel for calling it off. Not brave at all. And I would thank him heartily if I could."

He turned forward and didn't look at her again. Couldn't look at her again.

But when she sat back in her seat, he said conversationally, "Would you care to take a stroll with me after the lecture? With your maid, of course."

"I would love it."

Miss Blackstock opened her umbrella, hoping to protect herself from the Manchester drizzle. Her maid trailed a few feet behind them, and George wondered just how a tiny mouse of a woman was supposed to keep her mistress safe from any man who didn't want to be a gentleman.

Miss Twiggy said, "So, tell me about your three brothers, your father."

He groaned and she chuckled wickedly. "You don't get along?"

"No. At least not with my father."

She waited.

"He has plans for me. Has always had plans, even before I was born."

"They disagree with your own?"

"I don't have any plans." George nearly stopped when he admitted to it. Why it was so shameful, he didn't know, but he felt heat flood his face and he cleared his throat. "My father's plans have always been there, right in front of me. Perhaps having no plans at all was the only way I felt I could have my own."

"So what are these diabolical plans of his?"

"Oh, I suspect anything less than archbishop will disappoint him."

She laughed, and then realized he'd been completely serious.

He said, "My father has grand plans for all his sons though I suspect he is destined to disappointment regarding me. Have you ever felt, Miss Blackstock, like you were living a lie? That every day another piece of the real you was being sloughed off, and that one day you would wake up and there would be nothing left at all?"

She tripped and he grabbed for her elbow, catching her before she could fall. She looked up at him, the umbrella forgotten and the drizzle coating her stricken face.

She whispered, "Yes," and he hauled her up.

"Forgive me. I did not mean Mr. Moffat. I wasn't thinking at all."

He picked up her umbrella and her maid came to fuss over her mistress and Miss Blackstock stood there in the rain letting them.

When she was put to rights and they finally began moving again, George said, "Enough about me, I think. What of your family?"

She laughed weakly. Humorlessly.

"I don't know that my father ever had any plans for me but I think it's safe to assume I have not achieved them."

"And your mother?"

"I loved her."

George said quietly, "That is a lovely epitaph, Miss Blackstock."

She adjusted her umbrella and cleared her throat. "She spent her life trying to give my father a son and died doing it. And when she died. . .I wanted to die, too. My aunt came to take care of me and stayed when my father remarried. And when my father's new wife gave birth two years in a row, I left to live with my aunt permanently."

They walked a ways in silence before George asked, "And they've been good to you?"

"Better than I deserve. They've treated me not as a child but as an equal. As an adult."

"Sounds wonderful."

She nodded. "There is a kind of peace one feels when the people who know every one of your ugly secrets loves you. When they would follow you to the ends of the earth to help you get back what you lost. Good people who would give up their comforts, their home, their souls for you." She said softly, "I wish with all my heart that it had been enough to know that they would have and had not actually required them to do it."

George helped her across a busy street, his hand lingering on hers.

"Manchester is fairly terrible. But I am glad you left London, even if it cost your aunt and uncle their souls."

She smiled at him, the stricken look that had remained in her eyes since she'd tripped finally fading.

She took her hand back slowly and said, "Mr. Clarke followed you to Manchester. You must know the cost family will sometimes pay."

"Only too well. He reminds me of all he left behind in London with regular consistency."

And he decided right then to share his ugly secrets with her.

Because he knew hers. Her broken engagement.

And he wondered what she would say about his odd family when she had her own.

"Though, he had little say in moving to Manchester with me. Mr. Clarke's father was a farmer and he is my valet as well as my brother-in-law."

She looked at him with surprise, but he was gratified to find no censure.

"That is not a relationship you hear of everyday."

"No." George shook his head. "I loved his sister, and

when she married my brother it helped to have Collin with me. It helped to not be alone even if it sometimes hurt to look at him."

Miss Blackstock tilted her head to the side and studied him. "You loved his sister, and she married your brother."

George nodded.

"Your eldest brother," she said as if that explained it, and he laughed. The first time that he'd ever laughed at his broken heart.

"No. My twin."

She sucked in a quick breath and George answered before she even asked.

"He's not anything like me."

"Then perhaps she was the brave one. Painfully, heartbreakingly brave. And I would thank her heartily if I could."

George smiled at his own words. And knew when he deposited at her home that he wouldn't ever want to get off this path.

And the next evening, sitting down to dinner next to Miss Blackstock and across from Mrs. Turpin, Mr. Turpin at the head of the table and Collin diagonal, George was even more certain.

Dinner was a close and comfortable family affair; he and Mr. Turpin happy to talk cigars– the flavors, the brands, their favorites.

And he grinned when both Collin, "Not at the table, please," and Mrs. Turpin, "After dinner, we will leave you and Mr. Turpin to smoke all you like, Mr. St. Clair," interrupted them.

Miss Blackstock smiled. "Now you know. Should you ever tire of anyone's company, simply bring up the subject of cigars and they will banish you themselves."

"I will remember for the next time I visit with my father."

Mr. Turpin spoke up. "Is your father a vicar as well, Mr. St. Clair?"

Collin threw a long glance at George, who said carefully, "My father is the Viscount St. Clair."

Mrs. Turpin froze with her fork half-way to her mouth and Miss Blackstock said slowly, "I suspected you were the son of somebody. I didn't expect. . .that."

George felt a tad gratified that his father's title was so unwelcome; he'd thought the same thing himself a time or two.

"We all have our embarrassing relations. Remember, *I* am only a vicar."

Miss Blackstock said, "We could hardly tell, tonight."

"I don't have to be condescending and self-righteous *all* the time."

"I'm simply surprised you can turn it off. You being a vicar *and* a lord's son."

Collin nodded agreeably with her and George said to the both of them, "I can only turn it off when I am in the most agreeable of company."

Mr. Turpin smiled at the pretty compliment to his niece, though Mrs. Turpin still seemed shaken.

Miss Blackstock cocked her head. "You must mean my aunt and uncle then because you have been disagreeable oft enough in my company."

Collin snorted into his drink, sending himself into a short coughing fit, and Mrs. Turpin's color rushed back into her cheeks after the apparently devastating news of who George's father was.

"Oh, Mr. Clarke," she cried and patted Collin's back solicitously as he continued coughing.

George watched, smiling, and said, "I must mean them."

Six

Before the ladies left the dining room to the men, George nodded at Collin. Collin sighed, spared a glance for Miss Blackstock, then, finally, nodded.

Giving his blessing, and George smiled at his friend and then swallowed.

George helped Miss Blackstock with her chair and when Collin distracted Mr. and Mrs. Turpin with a question, George quickly followed her out of the room.

"Miss Blackstock, my father is. . .difficult. There's no getting around that."

She continued to the sitting room, saying over her shoulder, "I have never met a father who wasn't."

"Met many, have you?"

She quoted the bible, proving her point. "*And, ye fathers, provoke not your children to wrath. . .* Ephesians 6:4."

George took a breath. "Every vicar's wife should be able to quote the bible."

Miss Blackstock froze, then whirled around to stare at

George. "Is that a requirement nowadays for the Church of England? I hadn't realized."

"I hadn't realized there were any requirements at all. They approved me, a man who doesn't even pray," he confessed. Because he wanted her to know.

"A vicar who doesn't pray?"

"I suspect there is a range of vicar and they all have their own vices. Ingratitude is mine."

He came to stand right in front of her and she chuckled softly. "Is that what you call your failure to pray? Ingratitude?"

"I call it a great many things. Necessary being the most important."

"Why?"

"Because the last thing I prayed for was the death of my brother. God doesn't need to hear anything more from me."

She lifted her hand and grazed the side of his cheek with one finger and when he caught it gently, he held it to his chest.

He looked into her bright eyes– how could he have ever compared them to mud– and asked, "Does that make you hate me?"

She flattened her palm over his heart and said softly, "It makes me feel a great many things for and about you. None of them are hate."

"You should know what kind of man I am, Miss Blackstock. I want you to know."

She smiled at him. "And you're the wicked vicar? Mr. St. Clair, I already knew you were. It was a wicked thing to do, to make me dream of you."

He closed his eyes and she whispered, "George?"

"Hmm?"

"Are you going to kiss me?"

"I'm thinking about it."

"Stop thinking."

"If I kiss you, Miss Twiggy, I will then have to deposit myself in front of your uncle."

"You want to kiss him, too?"

"If I have to."

He opened his eyes to find hers smiling back at him, and George hadn't realized eyes could.

She said, "I don't think he will require it."

"I'm relieved. And unafraid."

"That's. . .odd."

"Do you want to know why I am unafraid?"

"You want to tell me, and I have no objection to hearing it."

"Your eyes are not shy and your smile is not demure. Your eyes are determined."

There was no giving Miss Blackstock to anyone. She would choose, her alone. She would choose. . .him?

"And I try so hard to hide the determination. What a pity I did not succeed. But tell me, Mr. St. Clair. What of my smile? What does that say about me?"

He looked at her lips and said softly, "Twiggy. So very twiggy."

Her lips opened and her determined eyes softened and George said, "Perhaps a short engagement. I can't wait to find out what I've married on my wedding day."

She agreed with a nod. "A short one."

George smiled. "Was that a yes?"

"Was that a question?"

"Yes."

"Then. . .yes."

George's heart started beating again and he leaned toward her.

"It was a wicked thing to do, Twiggy. To make me fall in love with you."

She whispered, "Did I?"

He put his lips against hers and whispered back, "Oh, yes. My Letitia."

Her uncle did not require kisses, though George did offer one to her aunt.

Letitia kept her arm linked tight with his as they celebrated with glasses of wine and when Collin congratulated them, there was real happiness in his voice.

"I think you will make my friend very happy, Miss Blackstock."

"Thank you, Mr. Clarke."

And when they left too late that night, Miss Blackstock's uncle returned the favor and distracted Collin while Miss Blackstock followed George out into the darkness, shutting the door softly behind her.

Her hand found his, her skirt brushed his leg, and her breath puffed against his cheek.

He closed his eyes, wrapped his arm around her waist and kissed her, and he *was* happy.

When he opened his eyes again, they'd adjusted to the darkness and he could see the smile on her face. See her happiness as well.

"Letty?"

She pulled back. "Yes, Georgy?"

"Twiggy?"

Her fingers grazed his lips and she whispered, "I like

Twiggy."

"So do I."

"I like you."

"I rather gathered that when you agreed to marry me."

"I don't know *why* I like you. And to be honest, I don't know why you like me. Not this me, the real me."

He wasn't entirely sure either. Except he thought she might have been made just for him.

Made to stand toe to toe with him.

He said, "We'll think on it, and perhaps have an answer before we actually wed."

She leaned against him, whispering in his ear and slipping something into his hand. "Maybe this will help. You did say a short engagement?"

He nodded, feeling her cheek slide smoothly against his own and realizing the item she'd given him must have been the twig that had once again been in her hair.

He let go of her, putting her bodily away and reminding himself that he was a man of the cloth and the walk home would do him good.

Reminding himself yet again that they were going to have a *very* short engagement.

Twiggy called out softly, "I'll dream of you tonight. And figure out why."

George decided abruptly that he and Collin would take the long way home.

Honora stayed outside in the dark.

Stayed outside and pretended she could see him walking down the lane for far longer than she actually could.

She closed her eyes and remembered how he'd told her he'd fallen in love with her.

Not the first time a gentleman had proposed the idea to her, not even the first time she'd believed it.

She remembered his non-proposal, and she believed for the first time that sometimes no words were needed.

She was still smiling when she went inside, still smiling when she bid her aunt and uncle a good night.

Her aunt stood. "Honora?"

"Yes, Aunt Gertrude?"

"Aunt Beatrice. Uncle Arnold. Have you forgotten?"

"Of course not. You know I try to stay in character."

"I don't think you've been in character for quite a while."

Honora hadn't been. And it was as if she could breathe for the first time in years.

"I don't need to be in character as Miss Blackstock. This is who he knows me as."

"I'm not talking about him. I'm talking about you. You are forgetting that this isn't real."

Aunt Gertrude glanced at her husband and he rose, saying, "I think I'll go see about some tea."

Uncle Hubert shut the door behind him and Honora remained standing, the smile on her face and in her heart fading.

The silence lengthened and both women waited for the other to speak. When Honora finally did, it was with gut-wrenching honesty.

"I don't want to play the game with him, Aunt Gertrude. He's not. . .he's not like the rest."

The older woman closed her eyes. "No, he's not. His father is a viscount."

The son of somebody. Somebody important.

Honora had known just by how he expected the world to fall into line around him.

She said softly, "We don't have to swindle him," and her aunt opened her eyes.

"Good, good. Call it off. Tomorrow. Tonight!"

"I mean that I could marry him."

She remembered his lips on hers and her hand in his. The countless afternoons they'd sat next to each other, bickering and trying not to laugh, and Honora thought a lifetime of that would be wonderful.

It seemed like a future one could welcome.

Her aunt sat suddenly, heavily.

"Honora, you can't get married as Miss Letitia Blackstock. It wouldn't be *legal*. She doesn't exist."

"It wasn't legal for me to become engaged under countless names, to collect reparations under those names."

Her aunt whispered, "You must see that this is different. Must see the consequences of such an act would not mean disaster for us but for your children. If it were found out that you'd married under a false name, they would be illegitimate. They would have nothing. Be nothing. And there would be no hiding it, not like last time."

Oh, it hurt. As it was meant to, and Honora could only forgive her aunt because there was just as much pain shining in the older woman's eyes at that hateful reminder.

The woman who had cried with Honora when first her mother had died– Honora only fifteen and still in need of a mother even if she wished she didn't. The woman who had cried her own tears over the death of her sister.

The woman who had held Honora again when her father had remarried– those tears hot and angry.

And then, finally, when Honora had discovered that a man could lie and take advantage of that loss and anger and guilt, promising the sun and moon and stars only to steal her virtue and her honor. Leaving her to discover that he was already married and that her child would never have a last name.

Those tears had been filled with fear. Those tears had been helpless. And her aunt had wiped them away gently, crying her own even as she made plans to protect her niece. Even as she stood between Honora and Honora's father as they screamed and shouted at each other for months, the whole family hidden away in the country until the birth.

Honora had stopped screaming when her stepmother had taken the baby from her body.

Had stopped shouting when the baby was given a last name and a family. A mother and a father and sisters. A future.

But Honora hadn't stopped crying, not for a long time. And when her father and stepmother had finally moved back to town, her littlest "sister" nearly six months old and her stepmother pregnant again, Honora had talked her aunt and uncle into renting a cottage far, far away.

They'd lived simply on the small portion Honora had inherited from her mother and when the tears had finally stopped, anger had taken its place. White-hot rage at a world that made women helpless and useless and worthless, and Honora had sworn she would never be helpless again, even if she had to steal her security pound by pound and man by man. Again and again until she could only remember who she was in the midst of strangers.

Until she'd accidentally found a man who could love her as herself.

She hadn't believed such a man existed.

Honora whispered to her aunt, "He knows *me*. He likes *me*. *Loves* me. It shouldn't matter what name I go by."

"Then tell him the truth."

Honora closed her eyes and the lies she'd been happy believing came crashing down.

He wouldn't love her if she told him the truth. And that must mean he didn't love her now. Couldn't, not when he didn't really know who she was.

Aunt Gertrude said, "*We* love you. We have sold our very souls to the devil for you. But this we can not do for you. We will not, because it is not *our* souls we would be casting away but your children's."

Honora opened her eyes and whispered, "I can't tell him the truth. He'll hate me."

"I know it. Know he won't forgive you the lies no matter if he finds out now or in twenty years. Know that his *father* won't forgive us." Aunt Gertrude clutched at her neck. "You should have said no. You can't marry him and we can't swindle him, not without risking swinging from the nearest tree."

Honora should have said no when she'd realized he was different from the rest.

But she'd wanted him. Wanted him still.

Wanted to marry him. Wanted to have children and a home with him.

Wanted him to call her by her real name.

"You'll have to call it off. Tomorrow. Tell him–"

Honora turned toward the door. "I know what to tell him."

All she had to tell him was the truth.

She'd had a child out of wedlock.

No good man would marry her after that. No vicar either, even one who didn't pray.

Her aunt said quietly, "We'll leave this dreadful town. Go somewhere warm and dry."

Honora didn't answer, merely opened the door and left the room, climbing the stairs to her room without a lamp and shutting herself up in the darkness of her room.

She didn't throw a tantrum. There was no wailing and gnashing of teeth. It wasn't a Miss Blackstock performance.

And she didn't go downstairs to be comforted by her aunt. To have the tears wiped away gently by someone who loved her despite everything.

Because this was a private release of all the despair a woman could hold within herself.

A woman who had been forced to accept the truth. A woman who had lost any hope of a family and a future for herself.

This was how Honora cried now.

In the dark. Quietly. With her tears sliding so slowly down her cheeks it was as if she was loathe to let them go at all.

Honora didn't sleep.

She tossed and turned, and came to the conclusion sometime near morning that she only had two options.

One, call it off. Tell him she didn't love him and never had and end it.

Or two, tell him everything. The child, the lies, her name. And hope that he loved her more than all of that.

And the only reason she could think any sane woman would pick option two was if she was pathetically and hopelessly in love.

Because if she did tell him, there were only two reactions he could have.

One, he would refuse to have any contact with her ever again.

Or two, he would hate her and do everything in his power to destroy her.

There wasn't even a sliver of a chance that he wouldn't care that she had lied every moment they were together. Had lied about who and what she was. Had lied to half a dozen men before him.

Not a prayer that he would take her hand and say, "Honora? I never liked the name Letitia anyway."

She steepled her fingers over her flat stomach. The stomach that had bulged with another man's child.

All she had was a single flickering hope that he truly loved her and would forgive her her sins.

And the only reason she would risk everything for that hope was because she was quite pathetically in love with him.

George didn't come in the morning, and Honora paced. Wishing he would come sooner rather than later, and then wishing that he wouldn't come at all.

Aunt Beatrice and Uncle Arnold– there was no reason to stay in character now– packed the rest of the house up, leaving the sitting room for last. For after.

Whether Honora decided to tell him the truth or just simply end it didn't matter to them. They would all be leaving Manchester anyway.

It was only Honora who had a choice to make. Only Honora who had any options and it made her laugh when she realized it.

A woman with options.

It was as horrible as having none because she couldn't decide. Telling herself one minute that she couldn't tell him and the next that she couldn't not tell him.

Her stomach was a mess and her temper was thin and she waited impatiently.

It was her experience that a newly engaged man visited his fiancé the day after. Always.

So she waited, and paced, and flung her hands out wildly as she fought an invisible foe, and when his knock finally came, she fell into a limp pile on the sofa, exhausted before it even began.

Her aunt and uncle entered the room, came to stand with her in her time of need as they'd always done, so Honora pushed herself to her feet, as ready as she'd ever be.

The housemaid led George into the room and then Mr. Moffat walked in right behind him.

Aunt Beatrice gasped and Uncle Hubert took a step forward.

Honora stared at George and he stared back, not saying a word.

Mr. Moffat said, "Good day. I almost feel as if introductions are in order again. Or for the first time, really. I can't call you Miss Blackstock, can I?"

Honora's stomach dropped.

Mr. Moffat continued on conversationally, "I received a letter a while back on behalf of Mr. St. Clair, wondering if I had could spare any information regarding a Miss Letitia Blackstock. Apologetically, of course, considering our sad history but any help would be appreciated and *might* lead to a happy ending for the lady. What gentleman wouldn't jump at the chance to redeem himself?"

He smiled. An ugly and frightening lifting of his lips that showcased the anger in his eyes.

"I sat down to answer it at once and realized just how little I knew of you. I didn't know your father's name, only your uncle's. I didn't know where you were born besides that it was someplace north of London. Did you know that quite a bit of England resides north of London?"

He laughed hollowly. The sound of a man who finally knew what a fool he'd been.

"And the more I tried to remember about you and us, the more I wondered why I didn't know where my fiancé was from. I certainly remembered where your solicitor was located."

There was anger in Mr. Moffat's eyes and righteous fury in his voice. They'd played him for a fool; they'd stolen his honor and his money.

Honora looked only at George.

Mr. Moffat said, "I thought it was only because we hadn't yet finalized the marriage settlement. We would get around to it and in the meantime you were enjoying shopping for your trousseau and discussing flowers, and I was happy to accommodate you because I was marrying a nearly perfect woman."

George moved then, blinking rapidly. His eyes softened and Honora almost thought that he was going to smile at how "perfect" Miss Apple Blossom had been.

She almost imagined he might smile and laugh and call

her Twiggy.

Mr. Moffat turned to George. "Has she started throwing tantrums and baking–" He closed his eyes and swallowed hard. "Has she started baking yet?"

"Not yet," George said and the smile stopped before it started.

He looked at Honora and she closed her eyes against the anger filling them. She wouldn't get a chance to explain.

Wouldn't get a chance to choose.

And then she opened her eyes and took a step toward him because she had to try anyway. "I wanted to tell you."

Mr. Moffat snorted. "Lord, how many times have you done this? Every move rehearsed, every contingency accounted for."

George said, "Is this rehearsed, Letitia?"

Mr. Moffat fingered a silhouette portrait hanging on the wall. "Oh, not Letitia. Not Blackstock. She was Dorine Calmly in Edinburgh. I don't know who she was before that, yet. I don't know her real name. Yet. But I believe a man should know the name of the woman who ruined his life."

Honora watched him walk around the room, fingering every picture. He picked up a book and flipped the pages, and Aunt Beatrice's hand went to her throat.

George apparently agreed with him. He said, "Your real name."

She met his increasingly angry eyes and said nothing. She couldn't tell him, not with Mr. Moffat ready to take that real name to the nearest magistrate. She couldn't put her aunt and uncle at risk.

George's hat crumpled between his fingers. "You won't

tell me."

Honora said softly, "She's no more real than Miss Blackstock."

He turned away, heading for the door.

Honora opened her mouth and he stopped suddenly, not turning around but saying over his shoulder, "I wondered, you know. Why you never said it."

Why she'd never said she loved him. Last night when he'd declared himself.

"Georg–"

"Too late, Twiggy," he said, and he left.

Miss Blackstock and her entourage had disappeared during the night, Mr. Moffat felt it important to come tell George early the next morning.

The man ranted and railed against the injustice in the world, swore he would get back his money if not his honor, and swore yet again that they would pay. *She* would pay.

George sat in front of the fire and wondered if he'd feel less tired and more angry in a few months, when the shock had worn off.

He thought maybe if he'd lost money along with his heart that it would have been easier.

Money and a broken engagement, that must have been the plan all along, and he scolded himself for feeling even a smidgen of regret that they hadn't got to that part.

Rehearsed. Everything had been rehearsed.

And he couldn't believe it. Not yet.

Collin finally shooed Mr. Moffat out and then set a cup of tea down beside George. He tiptoed out of the room without making any kind of snide remark about Miss

Blackstock, and George knew he must look pitiful.

Again.

Love had destroyed him again.

Mr. Moffat returned a few more times but when he could get nothing useful out of George, returned to London to interview anyone She had talked to– George didn't know what to call her. Not Miss Blackstock, obviously. Not Twiggy, too familiar for a woman he hadn't been properly introduced to. So she became She.

She.

Woman.

Deceitful, lying thief who'd stolen his heart and hadn't given it back before disappearing into the night.

George wondered if that had been the plan– to collect as many hearts as she could along with pecuniary payments.

Weeks went by. And then months.

George felt no less pitiable but he must have hidden it well since Collin began to act his normal self again.

Mr. Moffat kept Collin apprised of his progress. George didn't care, didn't want to know anything.

But when Mr. Moffat wrote from Bath telling the story of a haberdasher who'd got himself engaged to a woman who had loved hats, a woman who'd lived with her aunt and uncle, a woman who had been so excited to help but whose energetically awful designing abilities had made the haberdasher fear for his livelihood, a woman he still had fond memories of, and a woman he'd paid a nice sum to for breaking off their engagement and ruining every chance for her to have a happy and fruitful life, George was forced to accept the fact that Twiggy hadn't been the real She, either.

Another part, another character, and it was most likely she didn't even know who the real She was. Simply became whatever a man needed to secure his love, and then twisted that need until it was impossible for him to actually marry her.

George said dispassionately, "I wonder what she would have turned in to with me," and Collin gave him a friendly pat on the shoulder and offered him tea.

George sent Collin away with wave of his hand, realizing he must still look a little pitiful.

He must still feel a little pitiful because oh, how he wished she'd been real.

Wished that the woman who'd been everything he needed really existed.

York

St. Clair,

Forgive my penmanship. The twins insist that day is night and night is day, and will not believe a word I say on the matter. I suspect that one day, I will sleep a whole night through again. . .suspect it, but am far from assured of it.

Have you found a bride for your father yet? No, that's not quite. . . Have you found a bride for your father to happily object to? . . .You know what I mean. Write to me and tell me all that I am failing to ask.

Elinor sends her love, and don't snort at me like that.

Your friend, when he remembers his own name,

   . . .err, Sinclair?

Seven

It would not be an exaggeration to say that Honora's father was surprised to see her.

He'd walked into the drawing room with his mouth open and his face turning red. His greeting consisted of, "No notice that you were coming to visit? Has the post stopped delivering and I am unaware of it?"

"My letter must have been lost. I assume that's what happened to every one of yours these last ten or so years?"

Honora's stepmother, Fanny, stepped forward to hug her gently and interrupt their feud before it had a chance to start. "You look well, if tired. Was it a long journey?"

Honora nodded. "From London. On the train. My aunt and uncle could use a bath and a long nap."

Aunt Beatrice and Uncle Arnold could use a few meals and a few weeks uninterrupted sleep.

They'd run from Manchester, leaving what they couldn't carry and catching the train to Birmingham and then from there, to London.

They hadn't stopped looking over their collective shoulders until they'd been lost in the crowds and even then they'd hardly dared to venture out of their cheap and seedy lodgings for bread.

They'd argued and worried for weeks. Unsure of where to go. Unsure of just how much Mr. Moffat had found out.

They hadn't dared contact any of their banks and when the last of their funds ran out, they knew they'd have to leave London. Close an account and leave that day.

And go where no one could accidentally recognize them. Where they could have a warm bed and plentiful food and not spend any money until they knew they were safe.

Home.

And if Honora couldn't say the word without wanting to both sneer and cry, it didn't mean she didn't still have one.

Even if both she and her father wished it otherwise.

But The Very Reverend Charles Kempe was gracious to his dead wife's sister, their family beneath him but at least respectable, and he was grateful to them for taking over the care of his eldest daughter after her fall from grace.

He said to them, "You are welcome to stay while you are in York."

"How very welcoming you are, Father. I thank you for your condescension."

He pinched his lips together and she said quite convincingly, "We won't stay long. Adventure awaits us in Brighton but when I saw the train now came to *York*. . . I wondered what else had changed."

Not him, she didn't have to say.

Fanny took the older couple in hand, directing the

housekeeper to prepare a room and send a tray up, and it was then that eleven-year-old Temperance came rushing through the still open door and skidded to a halt. She blinked and blinked, staring at Honora hopefully. Her blond hair fell in ringlets down her back and her blue eyes were framed with long lashes.

She was beautiful, like her mother, and though Honora hadn't seen her since she was a toddler, she'd been described enough by her jealous younger sister.

That sister, ten-year-old Chastity, rushed in just behind her. Brown hair, brown eyes. Not beautiful but her inquisitive personality made up for it.

She was the one to ask, "Honora?"

She was the one to jump forward, to wrap her arms around the sister she'd only ever written to, only ever been told about.

And then Temperance came forward, too, and Honora could drop to her knees, squeeze the two young girls in return, and wonder how she would ever be able to force herself to leave them again.

Aunt Beatrice and Uncle Arnold retired gratefully and her father escaped his female brood the moment he could, but the girls hung on her and when Honora collapsed onto the nearest piece of furniture, Chastity squished herself between Honora and the arm of the sofa, refusing to move away.

Honora didn't mind, not in the least, even when Chastity turned to scowl at her and say, "You forgot my birthday this year."

"I am sorry, my darling. It was last week, and I did not

forget, but the packing" –the rushed and fearful packing– "forced it completely from my mind. I will make it up to you now that I am here."

She'd written every birthday since she'd left. From Bath, from Edinburgh, London, even Wales. When they had been far too young to even realize that she had left, that she had even existed, and Honora had always wondered if her father and stepmother told the children about her at all.

But as they got older, the return letters from her stepmother began to include snippets from the girls, and then snippets written by the girls themselves, and then individual letters that Honora had to assume never saw a parental eye.

Temperance complained about Chastity, and Chastity complained about Temperance, and Honora had known that they were truly sisters. That they were both loved and cared for. They were both safe and fed and warm.

Temperance, on Honora's other side but not squished against her, said, "Was Manchester a grand adventure?"

"Err. . ."

Nine-year-old Faith, her hair blond and her eyes a warm chocolate brown, leaned against her mother's legs and said, "Did you find a husband?"

"I wasn't looking for one." And then she paused because all three of her young sisters looked disappointed. "But yes, I did find someone."

Chastity jumped up and grabbed Temperance's hand, pulling her from the sofa and dancing around the room with her.

"Did you dance with him?"

Temperance tried to keep up and say at the same time,

"Was he handsome?"

They laughed at each other and at the idea of Honora dancing with a man.

Honora said over the laughter, "No. Handsome men are too much bother."

"Oh."

"But he wasn't ugly, either. He was normal looking. A man you would walk by without tripping over your own tongue."

They flopped onto the floor in front of her, excited and wistful, and seven-year-old Frederick Charles sat down cross-legged next to them. He looked like a little miniature version of their father, brown hair and brown eyes, and Honora could only be thankful that his appearance made Chastity look less like a changeling.

Fanny moved closer, joining Honora on the sofa and putting Faith between them. "Is this why you've finally come home, Honora? To get your father's permission?"

Honora looked down at the ten-year-old sister who was not a sister and didn't look at her stepmother.

"No." She sighed theatrically. "Because I do not have a love story to share with you, only a tragedy."

Freddy's eyes got very round. "Did he die?"

"He did not die. He was a troll. A sour, grumpy troll and he is still living under the bridge where the beautiful princess found him."

Beautiful, blond Temperance looked skeptical. "Was the beautiful princess you?"

Honora leaned forward and spoke so softly that the children had to scoot closer to hear her.

"There once was a not-beautiful-but-not-ugly princess who loved picnics. Especially picnics on bridges with her feet dangling over the edge and water rushing beneath her. And every week she would find a new bridge and eat her bread and cheese and smoked ham and listen to the loud water. So loud it drowned out the rest of the world."

Faith jumped from the sofa to sit with her siblings and Honora said a little more loudly, "But one week, just as she was settling into a comfortable position, a grumbling at her feet interrupted her solitude and before she could jump up and run away, a large head poked out from beneath the bridge. It was a troll!"

The children jumped, and Temperance gasped, "Was he hideous?!"

Chastity squealed. "Did he smell?!"

"Yes. And of course. And he had a large bogie dangling from his nostril."

All three girls shrieked and Freddy laughed hysterically and Fanny shook her head. "Honora."

"He's a troll. It's *de rigueur*. And before the troll had even come all the way out from under the bridge, he snatched the princess up in his large, roughly calloused hand."

Temperance covered her mouth and mumbled, "Did she faint?"

"Did she faint?! She poked him with her parasol! And said, 'You do not scare me, you grumpy sour troll.'"

Chastity put her arm around her sister and said, "It's okay, Temp. The princess really was scared, she just didn't want the troll to know," and Honora blinked and then looked down into her lap.

So that no one could see that she really was heartbroken over what she had given up. That she just didn't want anyone to know.

Her stepmother covered her hand and squeezed, and Honora cleared her throat and channeled perky Miss Blackstock so she could finish her story.

"Well, the troll roared at the princess and he puffed his trolly breath in her face and she poked him again with her parasol. 'Stay back, Troll,' she said. 'And kindly put me down this instant.'"

"Did he?"

"No. He didn't. But he was a troll, so the princess wasn't at all surprised. And looking down into the rushing water beneath her, she realized that she had come for a picnic by the river and here she was, by the river, so she climbed into a comfortable position in the troll's hand, poking with her parasol until she'd made a nice flat area, and then she set out her lunch."

Freddy looked impressed. "Right there in the troll's hand?"

Honora nodded. "And the troll watched her with a stupid, confused look on his face because he'd never met anyone who wasn't afraid of him before."

Temperance knotted her eyebrows and Honora amended, "The troll had never met anyone who didn't *act* afraid of him before, not even when his stomach grumbled loud enough to make the bridge shake. And when he lifted his hand up to his nose and sniffed her freshly baked bread, the princess whacked him on the nose."

Her stepmother murmured, "I had no idea a parasol could be so useful a weapon."

"Then the princess said to the troll, 'I suppose you will want to share my picnic,' and he replied, 'I suppose I could just eat you.'

'Well, it is my favorite smoked ham so let me think

about it for a moment,' she said, and the troll laughed at her wit."

Honora stopped, remembering her sour troll trying not to laugh, and Faith said, "She should share."

Honora laughed. "She should, and she did. The fairly ordinary princess broke her bread in two and offered half her ham, and they ate their picnic, both of them surprised to find the other was good company. And when the food was all gone, the troll grumbled that it hadn't been enough.

"'No,' the princess said because it hadn't been. 'Should I come again next week?'

"And the troll sighed and huffed and puffed and finally agreed that she could come. The princess nodded and packed up her basket and when she was down on the ground once again sniffed and said, 'I would have come anyway.'"

Temperance said, "Did the troll want to marry her?"

"Of course he did. She was a princess, and she made him laugh when no one else could. And every week the princess brought her picnic to the bridge and they slowly fell in love."

The girls sighed and Fanny smiled and Freddy made a face, and Honora said, "But the princess had a secret."

Her stepmother shifted in her seat and Honora leaned forward again. "The princess wasn't really a princess. She was a witch! And when the troll discovered this, he covered his eyes so he wouldn't have to see her."

Chastity crossed her arms. "But he's a troll. That's no worse than a witch."

"Maybe if she hadn't lied it would have been okay. But there is one thing no troll will ever forgive, and that's lying."

The children thought about that and Temperance asked fearfully, "Are you really a witch, Honora?"

"I am the worst kind of witch imaginable. The kind of witch who doesn't visit her sisters and brother. The kind of witch who forgets birthdays."

"The kind of witch who doesn't bring presents?"

Honora nodded and whispered, "I am that kind of horrible witch."

Chastity jumped up. "But you said you would make it up to me."

"I will. And next month it is Temperance's birthday and she will be eleven and I will send a present and not forget because even if I am a witch who doesn't *bring* presents, I will always be a witch who *sends* presents."

Temperance said quietly, "Does that mean you're not staying?"

Honora nodded and Faith said, "I wish you'd stay forever and get married and have babies and I would hold them for you."

"Would you?"

"Yes."

"Well. If I ever get married and have babies, I will let you hold them."

Chastity said, "And stay here, in York?"

"If I can."

"When you're married, you won't have to live here with Papa and then maybe you won't make him so angry and he won't make you so angry."

"It's a possibility, at least. It could be that York is just too small for the both of us."

"You could live outside the wall."

Honora smiled. "Perhaps."

Temperance decided suddenly that the troll story was just a story and asked, "Honora, why *aren't* you married yet?"

"I've haven't met anyone I wanted to marry."

Fanny said knowingly, "Except for the troll."

Honora smiled sadly. "Except for the troll."

Fanny finally sent Honora to her borrowed room to rest from the journey and shooed the children off, telling them they would have plenty of time to visit later.

Chastity slipped her hand in Honora's, showing her to her room and then jumping up to sit on the mattress of the four-poster bed.

"I'm your favorite," Chastity whispered as Honora sat next to her and smoothed her brown hair and looked into her brown eyes.

Honora tried so hard not to show it. To not give any indication that she felt differently about Chastity than she did Temperance and Faith and Frederick, and she forced herself to ask why the little girl could possibly think that was true.

Chastity answered calmly, "Because you named me."

"No. Papa named you."

"But you picked my middle name."

Honora nodded because she had. "Chastity Hope."

"And that's why I'm just like you," she said with pride. "Papa says I am."

"Then you must be just like him as well."

Chastity nodded solemnly. "Yes. Hard-headed and very stubborn, that's what Mama says."

Honora laughed. "Your mama is very wise."

"She isn't your mama."

"No."

"Your mama died."

"Yes."

"You must have been very sad."

"I was sad. And angry."

"At your mama?"

Honora shook her head. "At God. For taking her away. At Papa, for letting her go, even if there was nothing he could have done."

Chastity leaned her head against Honora's arm, forgiving so easily her many, many sins.

"Do you think you could not fight with Papa and stay?"

Honora swallowed. "I can try."

Chastity nodded. "I'll tell him not to fight with you, either."

"Does that work? Telling him what to do?"

"It works on Temperance." She kicked her foot out. "It never works with Papa. He gets angry."

"Like you get angry when he tells you what to do."

"Temperance doesn't get angry."

"She must take after your mother."

"Yes. They are good and kind and sweet and slow to anger."

Honora laughed and said, "That sounds like a quote," and Chastity nodded.

"But you and me and Papa are strong. We'll protect them when they are scared and hug them when they are sad. And they'll love us when we are hard and remind us when we are prideful."

Fanny stopped in the doorway, raising her eyebrows at her wayward child. "Come, Chastity. Let Honora rest before dinner."

Chastity bounced off the bed, running to her mother and taking her hand and saying, "I think I'll have to fall in love with a troll when I grow up. He'll roar and everyone will be scared and I will whack him on the nose with my parasol."

Fanny nodded absentmindedly and told Honora what time dinner would be served.

Honora hedged, not ready to sit down to an entire meal with her father. "Aunt Beatrice is very tired."

"I'll send a tray up for Beatrice and Arnold."

"But not me?"

"Welcome home, Honora."

Honora did try to get along with her father when they sat down to dinner. But all she could think when she looked at him, was that he'd taken her daughter from her.

She knew that he'd done it to save the both of them, and himself, from the consequences.

And she still hated him.

And still felt pathetically grateful that he'd cared for Chastity as if she was his own.

She had no mild and easy feeling for the man.

He waited until their plates were full before he said, "I hear talk of a suitor. I think."

Fanny indicated to the servants that they would serve themselves and Honora girded her loins for a battle. For an evening of lectures and bible quoting and she considered for one long moment following the servants out the door.

But she'd come here. Thrown herself at their mercy, knowing they would never turn her away no matter what disappointment she'd caused them, and she knew, this was her punishment.

She watched the door swing shut quietly and said, "There was a man, at least. And there was interest, I think. But it's a new world, Father. A man can know a woman without wanting to marry her."

He snorted. "We are all aware. And that is not new."

Honora remembered one moonless night, George's arms around her and his lips touching hers.

It was a wicked thing to do, Twiggy. To make me fall in love with you.

She'd felt that night. Not hate, not the bitter raging fire in her veins for all men.

A different heat altogether, and if she could have married him, she would have.

She would have risked everything to tell him the truth, she told herself. And she wondered if she really would have been as brave as she was in her imagination.

"He was a grump and a troll, but his interest was honorable."

"A suitor, then."

She shrugged. "It was cut short."

And she'd have to talk with her aunt and uncle before anyone mentioned her grumpy suitor to them.

Her father said, "Cut short by your lies."

"We are all aware, Father, what one big lie I have carried with me for ten long years."

That silenced him and they looked at each other, unblinking, until he nodded and went back to his meal, cutting into his meat with force.

"It is for the best, Honora. You'd have to tell any man who wanted to marry you and then. . . how could he not but question your resolve."

She passed the gravy to her father before he asked. "Of course. I mean, the experience was so very rewarding. I can hardly keep myself from doing it again."

The Very Reverend Kempe drenched his plate with gravy, then stopped before taking a bite. "Your morality is in question, the very fiber of your soul has been corrupted. A fallen woman is more likely to fall again and any man who married you would not only question you but also your children. Were they his? Were you true? It would be an intolerable situation for both you and him."

"Especially if he was a vicar," she said and her father put his cutlery down with a bang.

Honora patted her mouth with her napkin. "He was a vicar. The troll. My erstwhile suitor."

Charles settled back in his seat, knowing she'd meant to insult him. And maybe he was getting older because he let merely it go and said, "Even better that his interest was cut short."

"The best. I know I can never marry, Father. We do not need to rehash this lectur– conversation."

"If I could undo your actions and give you the future we all want for you, I would. If I could give you a husband and children, even now, I would."

"I know, Father. It makes it very difficult to hate you."

And it did.

She smiled brightly. "But at least I can travel. And at least I have an aunt and uncle willing to accompany me. And pay for it."

"You have your mother's portion. You could live quite nicely on it if you economized."

"I was not raised to live simply."

"You were not raised for a great many things and that did not stop you, if I recall."

Fanny interrupted them. "I do envy your travels, Honora. How was London? And Manchester?"

Honora forced a small bite down. "It was enchanting. You simply must go."

And then she felt terrible because Honora's stepmother had never shown her anything but kindness.

Honora took a too-large gulp of wine and said with less bite, "The children would thoroughly enjoy the train. Though I would go north to Edinburgh. I enjoyed Edinburgh."

"Not Manchester, then?"

Honora didn't answer, hoping that was answer enough, and her stepmother said softly, "Perhaps you can go back to Edinburgh."

"I was thinking the continent after Brighton. Or someplace just as foreign and exotic, like Cornwall."

Her father shook his head. "I don't think the continent would be a good idea for you. They are too loose with their morals."

Honora folded her hands in her lap and closed her eyes, suddenly so tired.

"Father, is that all you see when you look at me? Seventeen years of trying to be good– seventeen years of *succeeding* at being good and one stupid moment and all is lost? You have not known me for the last ten years and still you think I'd fling off my clothing at the first Frenchman who cocked an eyebrow?"

He didn't yell but she flinched anyway when he said, "That is how sin works."

"I'm not asking God if He can forgive me. I'm asking

you."

His silence was his answer and Honora opened her eyes and pushed her plate away.

"Thank you for giving my mistake a future. A family. Comfort and safety when I had none to offer. I know you didn't have to. *The sins of the mother,* and all that."

Her father said with all the authority money and power and respect had given him, "That sin will not be passed on. There will be no opportunity. Not even one moment where she can be deceived and tempted. I will protect her as well as I failed you."

Honora rose. "And thank you for extending your hospitality to my aunt and uncle. To me. We won't stay long, a week at most."

Eight

The rain dribbled down the window and George watched it blankly.

So gray and dreary. Life.

But it continued on.

George had discovered that early on, and here he was discovering it again.

No matter how one felt about the matter, life continued on.

Collin pushed in the door without knocking, he'd probably brought tea, and George, for one bright moment, was grateful for his friend.

A true and steady friend, here whenever he was needed.

Collin held a letter in his hands, not tea, and George closed his eyes.

"It's from your father, George."

"Throw it in the fire."

He'd been so looking forward to writing his father,

months ago. To having the satisfaction of choosing a wife before the old man could.

To knowing that, no matter what his father said or thought, George had chosen his own future.

And now, he had nothing again.

No want or purpose. No reason to be anything but what someone else had long planned for him to be.

Collin dropped the letter on George's lap and said softly, "It's Henry."

George didn't wait for Collin to be ready, didn't pack anything, didn't stop to even think how long he would be gone.

And he was grateful to be so close to home. Grateful that it only took a couple hours of hard riding to be running up the front steps, hardly taking the time to throw the reins of his borrowed horse to the nearest servant.

He ran to his brother's room, stopping with his hand on the knob.

He didn't pray, just paused. And wished he could pray.

He pushed the door in and Lord St. Clair sighed in relief and then stood, looking as if he'd aged ten years. Old and frail and worn out.

And Alice, sitting next to the head of the bed, stared vacantly at a spot on the floor, tear tracks marring her face though no tears were falling right then.

She didn't look at him; he doubted she knew he was there.

Henry lay in his bed, his breath ragged, his face pale and ghostly.

Dying. Again. For the last time, it looked like.

Henry had been getting sick for years, closer to death with each episode, and George had never come before.

His father had never sent a letter like this last one.

Henry needs you. Please, come.

Short, no explanation. It had been more alarming than if his father had described every detail of Henry's failing health.

But it had seemed as if his father couldn't spare the time it would take to even write how bad this episode was, and George had come running.

Lord St. Clair helped Alice to her feet and she protested.

"I can't leave him."

"George is here."

"He's here?"

When his father nodded, she looked around the room, and then the tears started falling.

She whispered, "No."

As if a word could stop Death when he was waiting.

As if it was George who would swoop in and take the father of her children, the man she'd loved for years.

George had no power here. No way to speed or slow his brother's passing. No way to end his brother's misery. No way to end Alice's.

George was a vicar. Not for very long and not a very good one, but he knew what his duty was.

Comfort. Peace. As much as he could give to the both of them.

But he had none for himself; he didn't know how to give it to them.

Lord St. Clair gently guided Alice out the door and she called over her shoulder, "Please, George! Pray for him. Don't give up on him yet. Please!"

Her cries woke Henry and he stirred, groaning. He took a shallow breath, opening his eyes enough to recognize his brother and then closing them again.

"Comfort him, son," their father said as he pulled the door shut.

George pulled the chair around to face the bed and took up the vigil. He put his head in his hands and stared at the blankets so he wouldn't have to stare at his dying brother's face.

Henry spoke slowly, haltingly. "I'm glad. You came. I wanted you. To hear my sins."

"Henry–"

"Not you, the vicar. You, my brother."

George closed his eyes. "Then I will be forced to tell you mine and no man wants those to be the last words he speaks to his brother."

"Now or never. George. And I need. Your forgiveness."

"No, you don't."

"I loved her."

George whispered, "Not a sin."

"Not for you, either. I hated you."

George kept his head in his hands but opened his eyes and looked up.

Henry said, "Forgive me."

Emotion welled in George's throat and he couldn't speak, and Henry said, "I was Cain. You were Abel. You know, able."

Henry grinned slightly at his own joke and George shook his head, suddenly thinking of Twiggy. Suddenly thinking she would have something to say here. A quote with a double meaning. And he thought Henry would have liked her.

At least the her George had known.

"I was so jealous. Of your health. Your future. I, the elder. But treated. Like the younger. Like a child. I hated you. And when I. Had the chance. I killed you."

George sat up and folded his arms. "Then we are having a very interesting conversation."

Henry whispered, "I knew you loved her. And I took her."

The room absorbed his confession and the silence was so loud, the roaring filled every part of George.

The emptiness filled him.

The emptiness had filled him since the moment his brother had ripped his heart from his chest.

Henry shifted painfully on his death bed. "I should have died. Before it was too late. For you and her. Better for everybody now. If I just sleep."

"Better for no one," George said and scraped his chair back.

He stomped from the room. Past Alice leaning against the wall just outside the bedroom and weeping silently into her handkerchief. Past his father, sitting in a chair and staring blankly at nothing. He jerked when George flew past.

"Is he. . . Did you. . . Did you comfort him, son?"

George shouted, "No!"

He stomped down the stairs and out the door and didn't stop.

Wouldn't stop.

He'd keep on going until he hit the sea. And he wouldn't stop then, either.

Pray for him, George. Comfort him, son. Forgive me, brother.

What was he supposed to do? What?

Did they think he spoke directly into God's ear?

Did they really think he was a man of God? He wasn't. Only a man.

A prideful, lustful, greedy, vengeful man.

A man who'd hated his brother for so long, he couldn't stop. Not even now, when it was too late.

George didn't make it to the sea.

The graveyard stopped him in his tracks. His mother's grave called to him.

They would bury Henry here, next to her, and George lifted his head to the sky.

He took you. I asked and I begged and I cried, and He took you anyway.

And I raged and I cursed and I hated, and He didn't take Henry.

He paused before entering the consecrated ground, just a slight check, and then firmly planted his boot on the soil.

He wound his way toward his mother's headstone. Cold and empty and neglected for so long, and he didn't know what she could do.

Mother, your sons need you, and he'd said that once before. Right before she'd left them, right before she'd died, because she'd had no choice.

And he realized the emptiness had filled him long before Henry and Alice.

He squatted and pulled at the plants growing at the base of the stone.

"I can't pray for Henry now," he said to no one. "I don't dare; God has never answered any prayer of mine."

A bird twittered in a nearby tree and a cow bell rung in the distance.

"And what would I say, anyway? Let him live? Let him continue to suffer when all he wants is peace? When death would end his pain?"

No answer. Like always. And George fell on his rump, propping his arm on his knee.

No answer.

Only the birds chirping.

Only the wind rustling the leaves in the trees.

Only the cows lowing softly.

Only Alice weeping and his father mourning and his brother dying.

Pray for him.

Comfort him.

Hear his sins.

Be a vicar, when he would rather be anything but.

George picked up a little twig that lay on the grass, twisting it in fingers.

He still had the twig Miss Twiggy had given him. A token of her esteem, and he'd felt so stupid for cherishing it.

For thinking he'd loved her when she'd been lying about who she was.

Just like he was lying about who he was. Lying still.

A vicar, when he was anything but.

"It isn't the same," he said to the twig.

But. . .what kind of woman gave a man a twig as her favor?

What kind of man would cherish a twig?

And how would she have known?

And he wondered for the first time just how many there

had been. How many men had thought they'd found their future when they'd found her.

He still thought of her, far too often.

Still wished he could sit next to her. Here. And tell her about his brother and Alice. Tell her about his father.

Talk with her and tell her all the horrible parts of himself and listen for her censure and then, never hear it.

As if she already knew.

I don't know why I like you, she'd said. Sour, she'd described him.

George smiled.

He was sour. And he sourly missed her.

She didn't exist, and he still missed her.

George went back to his knees and worked once more clearing around his mother's grave.

Loving mother, devoted wife.

And then below that, hidden beneath the growth and neglect.

Thy will be done.

George stopped and stared, wondering why his father had added that. The man was not known for being humble, for meekly accepting what life handed him when he could just as easily play God himself.

Except he hadn't been able to save his wife. Hadn't been able to heal his son.

Only to work with what he was given.

To somehow know what was a choice and what wasn't.

How was one supposed to know the difference? How was one supposed to know His will when there was never any answer?

Only the birds and the cows and the wind.

Only a long-buried mother. Only a brother he loved and

hated.

And a woman he couldn't stop thinking about.

George. . .didn't pray, couldn't pray, but he whispered, "I'm not a vicar. I can't do it."

But, what else was there?

> *Behold the fowls of the air: for they sow not, neither do they reap, nor gather into barns. . .*

George looked up.

> *Consider the lilies of the field, how they grow; they toil not, neither do they spin. . .*

George looked down.

> *Wherefore, if God so clothe the grass of the field, which to day is, and to morrow is cast into the oven, shall he not much more clothe you, O ye of little faith?*

George stood up.

> *Matthew 6:26-30*

George sucked in a breath and heard nothing else.

Alice and Lord St. Clair were inside Henry's room when George climbed back up the stairs. They rose, as if to leave, and he stopped them with a raised hand.

He stood at the foot of Henry's bed and opened his *Book of Common Prayer.*

And for the first and last time, he comforted his brother and prayed for his healing and heard his sins.

For the first and last time, he prayed with his whole heart.

For the first and last time, he was a vicar.

He began, "Peace be to this house, and to all that dwell in it. . ."

Honora stayed in York longer than a week.

Three little girls had clung to her, crying and wailing, and Freddy's little chin had wobbled while he'd tried not to, and Honora had given in.

Her father wouldn't have been surprised by her lack of resolve anyway, though she did refuse to eat meals with him again. And after the first night she went without dinner, a tray had been sent to her room each evening.

There were many things she thought of her father, but he would not let her starve while she stayed under his roof. Would not throw her out if she wouldn't leave herself, and somedays she wished he was universally hard. That she didn't have to reconcile his care for her with his utter lack of respect.

But she stayed, and she stayed away from him. She surrounded herself with her sisters, brushing hair and tying ribbons and listening non-stop because they never stopped talking. She played with her brother, glad that her father had finally got the son he wanted more than anything.

Honora was allowed to take them out of the house as long as a maid and a footman accompanied them, and she knew her father hadn't been exaggerating when he'd said that he would keep Chastity from making the same mistakes her mother had. That there would be no opportunity for sin to enter his household again.

The maid and footmen sandwiched their little group today. Honora, Temperance, and Chastity had decided to take a walk atop the restored sections of the city wall–

Honora wanted to see the new Victoria Bar entrance that had been opened in the wall since she'd left and the girls had both been promised a small birthday gift.

The girls chatted happily and Honora pointed out sights that were somehow both intimately familiar and long forgotten, and she nearly missed the gentleman leaning against the wall inside one of the circular tower outcroppings.

His hat sat squarely on top of his head and he read the newspaper as if he didn't have a care in the world and Honora's stomach filled with lead.

She stopped pointing and talking, tilting her chin down to hide her face with her hat. She forced herself to keep pace with her sisters and not turn and run like she wanted to.

They passed him, her sisters still laughing and giggling. One step, ten steps, fifteen. . .

And then a voice behind her called out, "Oh, Miss Kempe? How do you do?"

The girls stopped, turning to see who had called out, and Honora ground to a halt.

He knew her name. Her real name.

Honora turned slowly and faced George. She forced the dread from her voice before saying, "Why, Mr. St. Clair. You've found me."

He folded his paper and took a step forward and Honora took an involuntary step back. She murmured to the footman, "Take the girls ahead. I'll only be a minute."

When the footman hesitated, she said with a guileless smile, "I won't stray from your view."

George pulled his hat from his head, sketching a slight bow, and the footman began herding the girls forward.

"You look well," he said.

"And you."

She looked behind her, making sure her party was out of earshot, then dropped her smile.

"Are you here alone or should I look for Mr. Moffat as well?"

George replaced his hat and motioned for her to continue on her journey. She hesitated, looking over the side of the wall, and he said, "Don't worry. It's too short of a fall for there to be much use in chucking you over."

She narrowed her eyes at him, then turned and began walking toward her sisters very slowly.

He joined her, saying, "Last I heard, Mr. Moffat was in Bath. He journeyed there from Edinburgh."

Honora forgot to breathe.

"He'd made friends with a haberdasher. Are you all right, Miss Kempe? You look pale."

She sucked in a breath. "Fine."

"Hm. How many were there?"

She didn't answer, her heart beating too loud for her to think of anything clever, and George tilted his head.

"Fellows you've jilted," he clarified, as if she didn't know what he was asking. And when she still couldn't answer, he frowned. "That many?"

"Why are you here? To see that I am punished for my crimes? I stole nothing from you."

"Didn't you?"

"We were engaged for but one day. No one knew."

"I knew," he said and Honora closed her eyes briefly.

George said, "I wanted to find you. The real you." He looked at the little party ahead of them. "This was not what I was expecting. The daughter of a dean? Well-off and well-cared for. No need for your charades, at all."

Need. Honora supposed she could have stayed and died living under her father's roof. It's what she should have done.

But every day, she'd watched her baby grow older and everyday she'd been able to breathe less and less.

Even now, she looked at Chastity and the rage built inside her breast. Rage at the way the world was. Rage that she couldn't do anything to change it.

Only rage at it, and hurt, and make those who would never have to suffer like she had, pay.

She said, "No need. Only a choice I made. How did you find me?"

"Would you believe that as soon as I wondered where you'd run off to, I thought of York? Realized that you'd spoken of York with longing in your voice and then it was but a short jump to conclude you might come here. Though if you had not been here. . .I don't know where I would have headed next. Perhaps to Bath like Mr. Moffat; forced to work backwards to find out from whence you came."

"It was very clever of you, Mr. St. Clair. I applaud you."

He smiled at her tone. "Yes, you sound quite appreciative. Are those your sisters?"

Honora whirled toward him, stepping in front of him and stopping them both.

She didn't know what she would have said. If she would have begged to keep her sisters, her family, safe.

She'd never thought, never, that anyone could have followed her trail back to York.

Never thought that if she'd been caught, anyone else would pay except for her.

But before she could say anything, George asked softly,

"Was it a hard choice?"

"No. I hated. It wasn't hard at all."

"Did you hate me?"

She didn't answer and he pulled his hand from his pocket. Held a twig up for her to see.

Her twig?

"It's a strange token," he said. "And I'm still wondering, Miss Kempe. Why I liked you. If you liked me."

He looked at the twig and she looked at him. He said, "I'm still wondering if any of it was real."

"Would you even believe me if I said yes?"

"Perhaps." He put the twig back in his pocket. "But I've not been eating consistently since I left my father's house and I am hungry."

She snorted, then looked down quickly. "And you hate."

He said softly, "Perhaps."

He started walking again, forcing her out of his path. "But mostly, I'm just confused."

Honora didn't follow him. She watched his back walk slowly away, looked at her sisters as they tried to get glimpses of Honora's mysterious gentleman.

Run. Run.

George turned and he murmured, "Honora."

Her real name.

He held out his hand to her and Honora said, "You know nothing about me."

He smiled. "It's not nothing. But it's not enough. I don't think I will ever know enough about you."

Nine

Honora took him home and fed him in her father's garden. An impromptu picnic and Chastity had whispered loudly, "Is this your troll, Honora?"

"Yes."

"I'd better go find a parasol," the little girl had said matter-of-factly and run inside.

George raised an eyebrow and Honora raised one in return. "It seemed a fitting description."

Fanny clapped her hands, sending her remaining children to search for a very specific flower in the organized beds. They ran around, searching and laughing, out of earshot but never out of sight.

George bit into his bread and butter, closing his eyes in near ecstasy.

Honora watched him. "You really have been hungry."

"My father has disowned me. I can only hope it is temporary."

"And took away your living, too?"

George shook his head. "That's why he's disowned me. I've given up my living."

Honora looked away. She'd never stayed to see what happened after her broken engagements. Had never wondered how they'd fared with family and friends.

She'd never cared.

George said, "And since you ask. . ."

He waited and she didn't and he said, "I gave it up because I was living a lie. And I am tired of lies at the moment."

He met her eyes over another bite of bread. "I came for the truth, Miss Kempe."

"The truth won't make you feel any better. Mr. Moffat wasn't the first, though I'd hoped you'd be the last."

"And I'd already known all of that. How many were there?"

"Counting you?"

"I would prefer if you didn't."

She smiled at him. Then stopped.

She said softly, "Mr. Moffat was the sixth."

He looked at the large garden, the house behind her. "But. . .*why*?"

Honora sniffed and shifted in her seat and folded her arms. And then she told him the truth.

"Because the six does not include the one who came before them all. The one who preyed on a lonely girl and stole her honor. A married man who'd lied about who he was and left her with child, left her alone to suffer in shame. You know what he stole from me when he took *my* honor? My life."

Honora watched the children running around and didn't look at him. There was no middle ground in their world.

An unmarried woman was either a virgin or a whore. And she didn't want to watch him realize which one she was.

She whispered, "No matter what I took from those six men, I never took their life. I couldn't have; not like mine was taken from me."

George asked softly, "Did you love him?"

"If I say yes, does it change anything?"

"Perhaps."

"I didn't. I was young and stupid. I was lonely and alone. . . I thought I was alone, at least."

A bird twittered in the branches above their heads and she said softly, "Does it change anything if I wish I had loved him? If I wish there had been a good reason for having to give up my child?"

George sighed, putting his bread down and pushing his plate away.

"What happened?" he asked with dread in his voice, because if anyone had a worse life than a fallen woman, it was the child of a fallen woman.

And Honora knew she was lucky. Lucky to know that her child was well-cared for. Lucky to know anything at all about her child. Lucky to feel the pain sear into her soul again and again.

Honora watched three of her siblings try to find a flower Honora suspected did not exist. In a garden that used to be hers, with a family she did not belong in.

"My father sacrificed his immortal soul, threatened his earthly comfort, and gave her his name. He lied. Do you know what it does to a man of God to have to lie every day? To never be able to confess his sin without destroying what he loves? He saved us both with his lies. And I will hate him and love him for it until I die."

The tears prickled and Honora said through them, "My stepmother took my baby as her own. Loved mine when hers wasn't even a year old. Do you know what it does to you when the woman who replaces your mother is selfless and kind and you hate her?" The tears were still swimming when she looked back at him. "Swindling half a dozen men doesn't even sting."

"I think that it must have hurt you, no matter what you say."

"Are you trying to convince me or yourself that I am a good woman, George? A good woman would have stayed here, under her father's roof. Become a spinster and hidden her shame. Watched her child grow. Reveled in each stab as her daughter called someone else mother."

"Why didn't you?"

"I wanted. I wanted more than the scraps a husband-less woman is allotted. I wanted freedom. I wanted to forget. And I wanted to hurt." She clasped her hands in her lap, careful not to squeeze them. Careful to be relaxed. "I wanted a life."

"Did you find one?"

She had. With him. She'd found a place where she belonged.

She didn't answer and George said softly, "Honora."

Her name, again. And every cold part of her warmed.

She closed her eyes, tightening them. Tightening every muscle to keep from throwing herself at him and begging his forgiveness. Begging him to love her when she was Honora and not Letitia.

"Honora," he said again, and when she opened her eyes, George was looking behind her.

At a dark-haired little girl peeking out from behind a

hedge, her face stricken and her tears flowing and her
hands clutching a parasol tightly to her chest.

Chastity was her mother's daughter.

Honora could see the accusation in the reverend's eyes
and she couldn't deny it.

The little girl had been *listening* to what she shouldn't,
been where she shouldn't, and know *knew* what she
shouldn't.

Honora had jumped to her feet when she'd seen
Chastity hiding behind the hedge and the little girl had
started running toward Fanny. Toward her mother, and
then she'd just stopped, as if she'd suddenly realized what
the words she'd heard meant.

George had murmured, "I'll go," and Honora hadn't
even glanced at him. Had only locked eyes with Fanny, as
if they had both been dreading this moment.

And then the nanny had been called for and Chastity
had been shepherded into the library before she could
speak, before she could ask, and now she stood, alone in
the middle of the room as if she didn't know any of them.

Charles motioned Chastity to him and she pinched her
lips together. "You're not my papa?"

He shook his head. "I am Honora's father. I am your
grandfather."

Chastity's shoulders relaxed and she went to lean
against his legs. He was still hers, even if his position was
once removed from what she'd thought it was.

But now, with someone to lean against, she could stare
holes into the woman who'd borne her. She could more
easily ignore the woman who'd raised her.

Honora didn't know which of them had it worse.

Chastity stuck her chin out and said bravely, "You were talking about me. With the troll."

Charles' head came up, a question in his eyes, and Fanny murmured, "Honora had a caller."

"When? Just now?"

"We were all in the back garden, together." Fanny watched the little girl who still wouldn't look at her. "Chastity had run inside."

Chastity muttered, "I needed a parasol."

"It was a good idea. He's irritated with me," Honora said, and tried to remember what else she'd said to George St. Clair. What other secrets she'd not been careful with.

But Chastity only said, "Because you're my. . .you're my. . ."

"Because I'm not your sister. I'm your mother."

And if a ten-year-old could express utter outrage, she did. She turned on Fanny and said angrily, with disbelief, "Then who are you?"

Fanny said in a breathless voice, "No one."

Chastity sucked in a deep breath, turning back to Honora. "I'm ten! You didn't tell me in ten years!"

As if ten years was unbearably long, and it was. As if a ten-year-old could understand why a mother would have to give up her own child. Why a mother would have to lie about it.

Honora was much older than ten, had been older than ten when she'd had to make the decision in the first place, and she still couldn't understand it.

"I couldn't tell you before."

"Would you have told me someday?"

"Yes," Honora lied. "When you were old enough to

understand."

Chastity looked up at Charles, her father but now her grandfather instead.

"Who is my real papa?"

A thief and a blackguard. A liar and a manipulator.

Honora jerked when she realized she could have been talking about herself.

And she wondered, for the first time, if there had been a reason for his lies, a reason he'd stolen her virtue.

She would never know; and she didn't particularly care.

Her father opened his mouth and Honora talked right over him. Lies, lies, and more lies when the truth could only destroy.

"He was a soldier, and I loved him."

Chastity looked back at her. "Did he die?"

"He did. He was brave and good, and he took care of his soldier-brothers like you take care of Temperance and Faith and Frederick. Because he knew that a brother was a brother because of love, not blood."

"Did he love me? Even though I was his blood?"

"I'm sure he would have. I *know* he would have. But he never knew about you. He died before anyone knew about you."

"He would have married you. If he'd known," Chastity said confidently, and Honora nodded, relaxing back against the sofa and wondering if lies could ever become the truth.

"And then you would have been my mother instead. . ."

Her eyes darted sideways, at Fanny sitting there quietly, her hands hidden in the folds of her dress and her calm face frozen.

Honora said, "And then I would have been your mother. Just the two of us. No papa, no sisters, no brother."

Chastity's eyebrows crinkled. "But we would have lived here."

"No. We would have been alone. Living on the other side of the wall because Papa and I can't live under the same roof without fighting."

Her father let out a loud sigh and Honora almost smiled at him.

"But, did it hurt you, Honora? To give me up?"

The tears came suddenly, unexpectedly, and Honora blinked ferociously.

"It hurt so badly that I have never recovered. I didn't want to tell you because I didn't want it to hurt you."

Fanny reached across to hand Honora her handkerchief, and Honora took it gratefully and said, "I didn't tell you because you had a mother who knew that a daughter was a daughter because of love, not blood."

Chastity looked at Fanny, her eyes filling with tears, and Honora murmured softly, "I didn't tell you because the one thing I could give you, you already had."

Chastity's voice was tight and small. "You're not my mother."

Fanny's tears fell unheeded and she didn't even try to stop them. "I am."

She opened her arms and Chastity ran to her, hugging her tight.

Fanny whispered, "And you really are mine, Chastity. As much as your sisters and brother. Mine, and loved."

Honora dabbed her eyes, hating her stepmother and loving her, and knowing those opposing feelings wouldn't ever go away.

Fanny pulled her daughter into her lap, cuddling her

tight, and after a few minutes Chastity felt safe enough again to philosophically say, "It does make sense. Why they're so sweet. And why my hair's not blond. Why they're pretty and I'm ugly."

Fanny pushed Chastity's hair back from her face, saying, "Never ugly."

Chastity made a face, looking at Honora and most likely remembering the story of the not-beautiful-but-not-ugly princess.

Honora said, "If I could have given you beautiful blond hair and sparkling blue eyes, I would have. But I think I passed on my parasol-wielding abilities, if that is any consolation."

Chastity cocked her head. "And the troll likes you."

The troll had liked her, the real her, and Honora smiled slightly. It was unlikely that he still did but she said, "Yes."

"And the soldier loved you."

"Yes," Honora said, the soldier apparently already a saint.

"And Mama loves Papa, and we're just like him."

"Yes." Honora met her father's eyes and said again, "Yes."

Chastity snuggled deeper into Fanny's lap and said quietly, "Am I going to live with you now? You and Aunt Beatrice and Uncle Arnold?"

Fanny's eyes widened and Charles' chest expanded and Honora shook her head.

"That choice was made a long time ago, Chastity. And it can't be undone. It will be easier if you forget. Easier if you think of me as your sister because that's what I am. That's all that I am. And you can't tell anyone, not even Temperance."

"But she's my sister! And I love her and she loves me."

"Which means you only lie to her when you absolutely have to."

Charles opened his mouth, then closed it, and Honora said to him quietly, "Thank you."

Chastity sat up suddenly. "Wait, if you're my mother and they're your sisters and brother, that means they're my. . .aunts and uncle!" She thought about that for less than a second. "Well, I'm not ever going to tell Temperance or Faith or Freddy. I'm not going to call them aunt and uncle!"

Collin was waiting for George in the tiny room of the lodging house they'd found.

That meant he'd found no work for today, and George handed Collin the loaf of bread he'd bought with coins he could ill afford to spare.

Collin tore it in half, offering George his part, and George held up a hand. "I've eaten."

Collin took a large bite and said around it, "Where?"

"Miss Honora Kempe's back garden."

Collin growled, then took another bite.

George sat down on his trunk, tucked into a corner of the small room and said, "I know your thoughts on the matter and I don't need to hear them again."

Collin narrowed his eyes, chewing ferociously.

George said, "I need to send a letter to my father."

Collin swallowed. "I hope he doesn't chuck it in the fire."

"I hope so, too. Because I have a valet to feed."

Collin slowly put down his bread. "You're going back to

the vicarage. Perhaps they haven't given it away yet!"

George eyed his friend. "I knew you thought I would return to my living once I found her."

"You're not?"

George said slowly, "No. I have another idea."

Collin leaned against the wall and crossed his arms. "You're not ever going back?"

"No."

"I thought that once you found the chit who'd stolen your heart, you would be able to resume your life."

"I know. And don't call her a chit."

"Oh, there are a few other things I could call her instead."

"You could try Miss Kempe."

"I'm afraid that wouldn't make it passed my lips."

They stared at each other until Collin finally shook his head and sighed heavily. "What else did you find out in *Miss Kempe's* back garden?"

"I found that I still don't know enough," George said and Collin closed his eyes. He swore, long and heartfelt, inserting a few phrases he must have picked up from the manual laborers he'd worked beside since following George on this pilgrimage.

George stood, opening his trunk and rummaging around for paper. "I'm going to tell my father what I'm going to do, what I'm going to be, instead of a vicar. Instead of his fourth son. Three is enough for one man."

Because his father did still have three sons happy to live their life according to plan. Henry's health had slowly improved and when George had left to find his heart, his brother had once again been sitting in his plush chair. Watching his children play and disappointing Death one more time.

Collin said, "I thought you didn't know what else there was?"

"I didn't. It came to me while sitting in Miss Kempe's back garden. It came to me as I was wondering how a woman, or a man, could have a future when the one they were born in to is taken away."

"Or thrown away."

"Or doesn't fit."

"They starve, George."

"I would have agreed with you last year. And then Sinclair came home and told me about his. . ."

"It's called trade."

"Fine. His trade. His successful trade." And if the word still left a bad taste in George's mouth, well, he was a viscount's son.

Collin said, "Might I remind you that his successful trade is in India!"

George nodded. "It did not escape my notice. I also met a woman who had scraped together a life and a living when very few women can."

Collin's mouth fell open. "You. Are. Joking. Scraped together!"

"My point is not that I want to follow in either of their footsteps but that there are options I had no idea existed."

Collin looked around the tiny room, then flung his arms out wide. "What options? They're not here!"

"No, they're not here."

Honora didn't get out of bed the next morning.

She felt oddly empty, as if she was floating. As if she

was watching her own life disintegrate around her shoulders.

As if ridding herself of all her lies had somehow deflated her.

A maid came to check on her and Honora stayed in bed, sending her away without unlocking the door.

Aunt Beatrice knocked, and Honora didn't want her sympathy. Didn't want her aunt to stroke her hair and tuck her covers around her. Honora didn't want to be comforted.

She missed breakfast, took no tea, and dozed.

She was awoken a little while later by Fanny knocking lightly on the door.

"Honora? Mr. St. Clair is here to see you."

Honora blinked the sleep from her eyes and said to the ceiling, "How strange. Did he bring the magistrate?"

A long silence greeted her question and then finally a key was put in the lock and her stepmother pushed the door in.

Fanny looked at Honora, lying listlessly in bed, and closed the door behind her. She sat down next to Honora's hand and said quietly, clearly worried about young ears listening when they shouldn't, "Why would Mr. St. Clair bring the magistrate to see you?"

Honora woke up the rest of the way, thinking she might give lying up for good. Her secrets were spilling from her at an alarming pace.

Fanny shifted, jostling the bed. "There has been enough drama in this household, Honora."

Honora closed her eyes. "I know. I'll leave."

"I think I would prefer the truth."

"You really wouldn't."

Fanny said nothing and when Honora opened her eyes again, her stepmother was looking down at the skeleton key in her hand.

"I was only a few years older than you when I married your father and everyone told me that you would be a challenge."

"I do so hate when I prove everyone right."

"I'm so sorry, Honora. That I was too young to be a true mother to you after you had lost yours. That I was too overwhelmed with Temperance to see that you were in trouble before it was too late."

Honora shifted uncomfortably. "You don't have anything to be sorry for, Fanny. Including marrying my father."

"I have everything to be sorry for because you have suffered, and I have raised Chastity, and not for one moment have I wished that I could change your fate because that would mean losing her." Fanny stood up and walked toward the door, then stopped. "Thank you for her, for my brave little girl who sees the world like no one else does. Her life was worth all you lost, Honora. But if you can have it back, take it. Be brave."

"I can't have it back."

"Then why is Mr. St. Clair here? With or without the magistrate?"

Ten

Honora didn't know. And when Fanny left the room, that question hung so heavily that eventually Honora forced herself to her feet to find out.

And when she entered the sitting room, George took one look at her and jumped to his feet to wrap his arm around her waist and gently guide her to the sofa.

Fanny went to the other side of the room, leaving them as much privacy as she could without actually leaving them any.

And the woman may indeed have been happy to raise Chastity but she obviously had no intention of giving Honora any chance to do it again.

"Are you all right, Twiggy?"

Honora looked into George's eyes. "It has been a trying couple of days."

"I'm sorry. If I'd seen her. . ."

If he'd seen her, Honora would have had a few more years most likely but their conversation would have happened.

The ability to be where one shouldn't was also something Honora had passed on to Chastity.

Honora leaned toward George and whispered, and was reminded of happier days when she'd sat next to him and whispered, "George, please. Whatever you've come for, let's get it over with. I am utterly exhausted."

He looked at Fanny, not very far away at all. Looked behind him at the open door.

"Perhaps we could go out to the garden. The sun will do you good."

"There's sun today?"

"A little. Would your siblings like to join us outside as well? I'd like to know where everyone is at all times."

"You've figured us out already."

He helped her rise. "I have."

The girls and Freddy were rounded up and they all went outside to play in the sun.

A blanket was tucked around Honora, as if she was an invalid, and she wondered just how terrible she looked.

How empty.

George sat next to her and when everyone was visible, yet far enough away, he said, "I loved a good woman once. Not you."

Honora smiled and closed her eyes.

"The clarification was unnecessary."

"I loved her, and I just sat and waited for her to realize that she loved me. I just sat and watched her marry my brother. I've been destroyed by love twice now."

You, and he didn't have to say that she had been the

second.

"You've come back for thirds?"

"I sincerely hope not. I came for the why."

"And I've already told you. A few stolen minutes, two lives destroyed, and very few options."

The bird twittered again and George waited until she opened her eyes again to say, "Minutes? Does it change anything if I wish you'd thrown away your virtue and future for at least an hour or two?"

She looked sideways at him.

He repeated, "I wish it had been worth it. I wish it had been worth all you suffered."

Honora watched four young children running in circles around their mother, remembered how Fanny had said Chastity's life was worth all that had been lost.

Perhaps she had been worth it.

George watched them too, and he asked, "*Was* your child's life destroyed by that minute?"

"Minutes, plural. You don't need to make it worse than it actually was."

"You don't need to make it worse than it actually is, either. Did you give her the best possible life out of very few options?"

Honora leaned toward him, the blanket suddenly stifling her, and she whispered hotly, "Yes. And I refuse to be so helpless ever again. I would do it all over– take bits of security from every man until I had enough. Until I would never have to make that choice again."

"So that is the why," he said and nodded. "Now I want to know if. I loved once, before you. And I still don't know what was true. If she'd ever loved me back. And I don't think she could even tell me, not now. So I want that truth.

From you."

She raised her eyebrows. "You want a liar and a swindler, someone you could have hanged at the snap of your fingers, to tell you that she really– *no, really she did*– loved you."

He took a deep breath, leaning back in his seat and closing his eyes.

He nodded again and she watched him for a long moment.

"What are you doing?"

"Listening."

Honora looked around, as if she could hear with her eyes.

"To what?"

"The birds," he said, and Honora could suddenly hear the twittering in the tree tops.

"The wind," he said, and Honora could hear the leaves rustling.

"The children," he said, and Honora could hear the giggles and whispers.

"You," he said.

"I love you," she said with all the disgust she could muster. "And it's horrible."

"Love is."

"I didn't mean to. You were going to be the last, a payment so large we'd be comfortable for the rest of our lives."

"And then you realized you could have more as my wife."

"And then I realized I could have *everything* as your wife."

And even she could hear that. The truth.

She could have had everything with him. And here he was.

She whispered, "Why are you here?"

He opened his eyes.

He didn't look at her, just stood up and adjusted his coat.

"Thank you," he said.

And he walked away.

Honora huddled beneath the blanket after he left, cursing all men.

George. The six who'd come before him. And the one who'd necessitated them all.

She watched Chastity running around, playing with her sisters, and thought maybe her stepmother was right.

She'd been worth all that was lost.

You can have it back. Take it. Be brave.

Be brave? She'd be angry.

George had come here and made her say the truth to him and then he'd left?

When he loved her, the real her, in return?

The only one who ever had, and he'd left?

Honora flung the blanket off and called, "Chastity. I need your parasol."

She'd go find him and poke at him until she had him right where she wanted. York was a small city; he'd found her, surely she could find him in return.

Her father called out behind her, "Honora," and when she turned, there was George standing next to him.

Honora blinked and Chastity ran up to say, "Should I go get it?"

"I don't know."

Charles called for all his children to gather round and held his hand out to his wife and when they were all in front of him, he smiled.

"I have given my permission to Mr. St. Clair to marry Honora."

Fanny gasped and covered her mouth, the girls squealed with delight, and Honora stood absolutely still.

". . .You said I could marry him?"

"We had a long conversation," he began and Honora sucked in a breath.

Her father continued over her. "And I am assured that not only does he know you very well, he also loves you."

Fanny pulled her handkerchief from her pocket and dabbed at her eyes. "Oh!"

"And I'm not going to say no to a viscount's son, even if he is currently profession-less. He seems like a man with a plan."

Honora finally met George's eyes and said, "He does?"

"Oranges. And cigars."

She raised an eyebrow at him. "Steam?"

George curled his lip. "Trade. But it is better than the alternative."

She whispered, "Marriage," and he smiled.

"It seemed better than the alternative."

When the girls had stopped squealing and Honora's stepmother had stopped crying and her father had stopped thanking God for his good fortune, George held out his arm to Honora.

They walked slowly around the perimeter of the garden

and when they were far enough away from young ears, Honora said, "That was the worst marriage proposal I have ever heard of; you didn't even ask me. I think you should do it again."

"How many times have you been proposed to, Honora?"

"Including both of yours?"

He nodded and she said, "Eight. And your two were, by far, the worst of the bunch."

"Eight is enough."

It was hard to argue with that even if she wanted to.

She said, "You could have told me instead of leaving me there, alone. To worry. To get angry."

"I've been plenty worried and angry the last few months. I find I am more petty than I previously suspected."

"I'll keep that in mind. For the future."

He glanced down at her and she said softly, "Forgive me?"

"Never. I will never forgive you for making me fall in love with you."

She swallowed, blinking back happy tears. "Petty, indeed. Haven't you ever read Matthew 5:7? *Blessed are the merciful: for they will be shown mercy.*"

He reached out, catching a lone tear with his thumb. "*Blessed are ye that weep now: for ye shall laugh.* Luke 6:21."

And she did.

She looked behind her, at her family watching them, and gestured at the flower beds as if they were talking about the garden.

She said, "They're never going to leave us alone, not until the marriage deed is done, or else this would be a perfect moment to kiss you."

"Since I am no longer a man of the cloth, that is probably for the best. You are far too tempting for me to be kissing before we're married."

"Father can get us a special license."

George shook his head. "No. No special license. The banns will be read and we'll do this right."

She lifted an eyebrow at him because they hadn't done anything *right* and he said, "Besides, it will give me time to hear from my father. I've proposed a business enterprise to him. If he says no, we'll visit him after the wedding so you can change his mind."

"Does this enterprise have something to do with your steam?"

"Our steam. We're going to America. If my good friend Sinclair can take his bride to India and send back trinkets, I can take my bride to America and send back cigars and oranges."

Honora stopped and blinked, and George said softly, "You can't stay here. In York. In England. Moffat will discover all your sins and then find you. A woman does not steal a man's honor though the opposite happens with regular frequency."

"And you're going to leave your home and family for me?"

"I am."

"Because you love me?"

"Because I never truly believed in God, or his love, before you. I studied and I knew the words and I knew what I *should* feel, but I never did. And then I found you and realized that He'd made you just for me. He made you hardened and cynical and unafraid. He made me heartbroken and prideful and slow to forgive–"

She pointed at a tasteful grouping of trees and started walking toward them, tugging him along. "You forgot sour."

He smiled. "Sour, too. All so that when I met you, I would be able to do anything for you. So that when I had a choice to make, I could recognize it. So that I would know the difference between no choice and a hard choice."

"America," she said slowly, never having considered it before. Then, "My aunt and uncle will be coming with us."

"I have family of my own that will need to be accommodated. Collin would benefit from an older, wiser touch because he seems far too interested in the idea of American women. Although, I don't see that they ever had much luck with you."

"Don't hold it against them."

"Oh, I think I've placed the blame squarely where it is due," he said and she laughed.

"I want Chastity to come to America, too. When she's older. When she wants to. When we're settled. I will never be her mother, I gave that up ten years ago, but I want to know her and I want her to know me."

And then she said, truthfully, "I'm afraid I don't even know who Honora Kempe is."

"And I don't think you should waste anymore time on it. It is of far more importance to me who you decide Honora St. Clair will be."

She pulled him behind the nearest tree trunk, sliding her hands inside his coat and pulling his body tight against hers.

He cupped her face with his hands, tracing her eyebrows with his thumbs and murmuring, "How was that proposal? Any better?"

She nodded, a smile transforming her face. "Much better."

"Was that a yes?"

"Was that a question?"

"Oh, yes. My Honora."

She sighed happily, going to the tip of her toes to meet George's lips with her own.

Her father called her name, telling them both to come out from behind that tree, and the children giggled loudly.

The wind whipped the leaves of the trees into wild applause, the birds sang, and the sun shone brightly down on them.

And she said, "Yes."

To George Sinclair, his wife Elinor, and their two lovely and (I am sure) wild children,

I am sorry, old friend. I will not be joining you in the east. I am, as I write this, boarding a steam ship to the west. To America.

One, it's a shorter (thirteen days!) and faster (ten knots!) journey. And two, they make better cigars.

I'll send you some with the birth announcement. Honora assures me there is no chance of that happening before the ship makes land, and she usually says it with cutting droll, so I am forced to believe her.

I am convinced you would love her– nearly as much as my Father does– which is reason number three we are heading to the opposite end of the world. I, at least, made certain your bride would never be tempted by me. Your friend, in love,

George St. Clair

* * *

THE RELUCTANT BRIDE COLLECTION

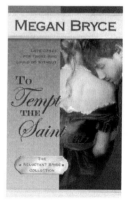

Available in ebook, paperback, and audio

www.meganbryce.com

A
TEMPORARY
ENGAGEMENT

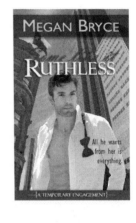

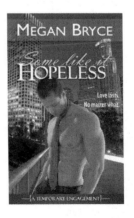

Available in ebook
and paperback

www.meganbryce.com

91982016R00094

Made in the USA
Lexington, KY
28 June 2018